MURDER AT THE CHÂTEAU

An absolutely gripping cozy murder mystery

ANNE PENKETH

A Brittany Murder Mystery Book 2

Joffe Books, London
www.joffebooks.com

First published in Great Britain in 2024

Cover art by Jarmila Takač

ISBN: 978-1-83526-635-9

For Lateef
"Expect the unexpected"

CHAPTER 1

For Alex "Rockface" Johnson, one of the pleasures of living in France was reading the local press.

He sought out the news items tucked away at the bottom of the page which reflected the eccentricities of village life. They usually involved animals, or drink, or sometimes both.

"Listen to this one," he said to his wife Vicky. They were seated at their dining table where she was spreading marmalade on to a croissant while watching the gardener prune back roses in the flowerbed outside.

Vicky picked up her phone to make it clear that she was more interested in checking her emails than the stupid human-interest stories in *Le Télégramme*.

"No, listen, darlin'. This is a good one: 'Panic as alpaca wanders into chemist,'" said Alex.

"An alpaca? Did it have a prescription?"

He read on. He was used to her put-downs. "Wait, it says it was in a village on the other side of Carhaix . . . I think there's an alpaca farm down there."

"Oh, so that explains why it goes shopping at the nearest chemist then." With a sigh, Vicky took a bite of her croissant and licked the marmalade before it dropped onto her plate. She'd long ago stopped being surprised at the weird

1

goings-on in their remote part of Brittany, where her rock musician husband had become a local celebrity.

He'd earned his nickname, not because of the deep crevices carved into his cheeks by years of drug abuse, but because his die-hard fans, including the French, knew him as the "face of rock". In middle age, he was enjoying something of a revival after performing at the annual rock festival in Carhaix. The locals had taken him to their hearts after he'd bought a ramshackle château and used Breton workmen for the renovation, instead of importing contractors from England. For her part, Vicky couldn't understand why it was taking so long to complete. Although she loved their turret bedroom and spacious reception rooms, she was annoyed that Alex seemed to accept the delays which meant that the dry rot in one wing was still awaiting attention.

She resumed her contemplation of the grand sweep of the grounds through the bay windows while finishing her croissant. The gardener was now bent over weeds among the roses, pulling them up with a trowel before throwing them on to the grass with the overarm grace of a ballet dancer. She watched as the handyman, paunch hanging over the waist of his jeans and his hair in a ponytail, sauntered past the flowerbed on his way to the barn and made a comment that caused the gardener to go red in the face. He, in turn, shouted something rude in the direction of the handyman, who was already out of sight. Vicky shook her head. This place had more drama than *The Archers*.

"Aren't you having one?" she asked Alex, pointing to the remaining croissant. "It's one of Pippa's. She's bringing the food for tonight."

His eyes still on the paper, Alex muttered, "Good." He'd organised a boar hunt in a thick wood that ran down the southern side of the property. It would be one of the last of the season, which closed at the end of March.

"What time are they coming?" Vicky said.

"About half past three, and then we'll be straight off. Jean-Michel is bringing his hounds." Alex stood up, leaving the folded paper on the table.

"I'm going to clean my rifle," he announced.

"And what about dinner? It would be helpful to know when to expect you all so I can get everything ready."

"It depends," he said over his shoulder. "It won't be late, though, as we're not allowed to hunt in the dark."

She knew what that meant. They'd be hours recounting their hunting stories over several rounds of drinks before sitting down to eat, so she was right to have planned a chicken dinner with no frills. Anything more adventurous would be wasted on that lot. She decided they could help themselves, and she'd leave them to it.

* * *

Vicky duly waved off the hunting party, all wearing hi-vis vests, in mid-afternoon. Alex set off on his quad, his straggly hair — channelling Ozzy Osbourne and Iggy Pop — flying in the breeze. Jean-Michel followed, with his dogs in the back of his SUV. The others, four Bretons and an Englishman, clambered into their vehicles, throwing their guns into the boot. Vicky knew there were at least two families of wild boar in the wood because they often saw them trotting along the drive like they owned the place, or rooting for buried acorns and beechnuts among the trees.

She returned to the kitchen where her friend Pippa was unloading canapés, bread and her famous rum babas. The aroma of warm baguettes filled the air.

"I hope they don't kill too many of those bloody *sangliers*," Vicky commented. "I've still got the remains of the last hunt in the freezer."

Pippa smiled. "They are a pest though, aren't they? The farmers are always complaining about them ruining their crops. I almost ran into a troupe of them when I was driving into Carhaix the other day."

"They're big buggers too." Vicky wrinkled her nose, freckled by the outdoor country life. "Dangerous."

"And these are the chickens and the veggies from Jennifer," Pippa said, laying out two large birds on the granite counter. "She's childminding tonight. She did mention that, didn't she?"

"Oh yes, she did when I paid her at the market," said Vicky.

"Let's see what else she's put in." Pippa took out carrots, potatoes and beans from a carrier bag.

"This is great. I'll roast the spuds with the chicken," said Vicky.

They got to work, Pippa preparing the vegetables while Vicky went into the dining room to set the table. On her return, she offered Pippa a cup of tea. As Pippa ran the bakery in the nearby village of Louennec, and was an excellent source of gossip, it was a good opportunity to catch up.

"Didn't I see Jean-Michel's car driving off?" Pippa asked, pulling up a chair at the kitchen table. "I didn't know he had hounds."

"I'm surprised you don't hear them barking," said Vicky. "Doesn't he live in the village?"

"Yes, but not near me. And when he comes in for his baguette, we usually talk about what's going on at the *mairie*, not his private life."

"He's one of the deputy mayors, right?"

Pippa nodded. "Yes. He tells me that it's pretty tense on the council at the moment. There's a ghastly woman who seems to think she's in charge, although Meredith is the actual mayor."

"Oh dear. That's tricky."

"Meredith is certain that it's because she's English, even though she's got French citizenship as well. You didn't know her husband, did you?"

Vicky shook her head, her hennaed hair glossy in the dying rays of the sun.

"Well, he was on the council until he died, and he couldn't stand that woman either," Pippa added.

Vicky had put the chicken and potatoes in the oven to roast. The two women didn't notice the time until Vicky switched the lights on and looked up at the clock on the wall.

4

It was 6 p.m., and the sky outside the kitchen windows was darkening.

"I'm going up to change," she said. "I thought they'd have been back by now."

"I'd better go," said Pippa, standing up. "I promised my apprentice that I'd do the prepping for tomorrow before closing up. She's holding the fort by herself at the moment. Are there eight of you for dinner?"

"Well, seven, actually. I'm the maid for tonight. I didn't fancy sitting down with a bunch of blokes telling dirty jokes in two languages. And I gave the cook the night off."

"You have a cook?" Pippa stared at her, evidently wondering why she had been asked to help out.

Vicky smiled. "I'm employing half of Carhaix here. Not only a cook, but two cleaning ladies, a gardener and a handyman. He's only part-time, but Alex likes him as he's a metalhead and a fan of his music. He goes round listening to 'Kill Satan's Child in the Cellar'. Do you know that one?"

Pippa shook her head. She'd never been into heavy metal, preferring female vocalists who sang about mental health issues. She always said that the sad songs made her realise that her own life wasn't so bad.

"This place is so big I could hire even more staff," Vicky added, "although it would be more work for me, as I'm the one who pays the bills. Alex just fixes their wages, which is good because they're always trying to get a raise, and I've told them not to bother me. And in any case, Alex's French is much better than mine, which is handy in an argument. I just wave my arms around. The trouble is that they're all at each other's throats, like rats in a sack. Ah, well, that's village life, I suppose."

Hearing footsteps on the stone floor, they both turned round.

"Here they are," said Vicky. She took off her apron, expecting to see Alex.

The door opened. Vicky recognised Derek, a doctor turned fitness instructor who lived in the village. His yellow jacket was covered in blood. Maybe the boar had put up a fight, she thought. Then she saw his sombre expression.

Something was wrong.

"Where's Alex?" she asked, her voice tinged with panic.

Derek moved towards her. Instinctively, she backed away and gripped the kitchen counter.

"I'm sorry, Vicky. He's been shot."

CHAPTER 2

Vicky gasped. Pippa went to her and put an arm round her shoulder.

"What happened?" she asked Derek.

"I'm afraid there's been an accident," Derek began. "I couldn't save him. The bullet penetrated his femoral artery, I think. By the time I got to him, he'd bled out."

"What do you mean 'bled out'?" Vicky cried. "Is he dead?"

She shook her head in disbelief, her thin fingers twisting her wedding ring. They heard the sound of sirens outside the house.

"I'm afraid so. I'm so terribly sorry," said Derek, assuming his best bedside manner. "That'll be the emergency services. And the gendarmes are on their way."

"You deal with it," said Vicky, sinking into a chair. Pippa wondered whether to switch off the oven. The evening's festivities were obviously cancelled, but the chickens and roast potatoes were almost done. She could hear Derek telling the paramedics where to find Alex who, he said, had been shot in the buttocks.

In the buttocks! Pippa glanced at Vicky, hoping she hadn't overheard. She was staring into space, lost.

Outside the kitchen, one of the medics exclaimed in shock, "*C'est Rockface*?" Derek said that it was.

He came back into the kitchen.

"Let me have your number, Vicky, so they can contact you," he said. "Vicky?"

She stirred. "Do I go with them?"

"They'll ring you," he said, and cleared his throat. "You'll have to identify the, er, the body."

The front doorbell rang. "I'll get it," said Derek. He returned with two gendarmes and explained briefly what had happened.

"Are you the hunt leader?" one asked.

"No. That was our friend, Alex."

"But you all have licences, *oui*?"

"Of course," he said. "At least, I presume that the others do."

They asked Vicky who had taken part in the *battue* to flush out the boar. She began slowly ticking names off on her fingers.

"Let's see. There's Jean-Michel, Armel, Pierre, Gilbert . . . who else? Did I say Armel?" She looked up at Derek. "Was there anyone else? I can't remember." She looked at them blankly. "I can't cope, sorry. You know them better than me."

"Did you forget Pascal?" he said. "Anyway, they're still at the scene," he told the gendarmes. "I can take you down there, if you like."

Pippa rang Gwen, her young apprentice, who offered to prep for the next day before shutting the bakery. Pippa was thankful that Gwen was so reliable as well as a good worker. Otherwise, it would have meant a late night for Pippa at the bakery, and even less sleep than usual. She'd never realised until she made her career-changing move to Brittany a couple of years earlier just how relentless the hours could be.

She rang off and sat with Vicky, who had lapsed into stunned silence, repeatedly wiping her hands on her jeans. Pippa was reminded of Lady Macbeth trying to wash away Duncan's blood. Could Vicky have a guilty conscience? Pippa dismissed the thought as ridiculous.

After a while Vicky said, "I can't believe this. I can't believe he's gone. Our last conversation was about an alpaca, for God's sake. I never even got to say goodbye to him!"

"How about a stiff drink?" said Pippa. "And the chickens must be ready by now. Do you want something to eat?" The delicious smell of the roast potatoes was making her hungry.

"I couldn't. You take them."

"No. Thank you. I'll wrap them for you — they'll keep in the fridge." The thought of wasting so much food was anathema to Pippa, who sold the leftovers from her bakery at knockdown prices on a phone app.

While Vicky watched in silence, Pippa took the food from the oven and switched it off. She went to the fridge and took out a bottle of Gros Plant, the local tipple.

"White OK for you?" she asked Vicky.

"Whatever."

She filled two glasses, handing one to Vicky, who grasped it with both hands, the sparkling nail varnish of the ageing rock chick incongruous against the sorrow etched on her face. She took a long swig.

"Derek doesn't seem like the hunting type, I must say," Pippa said from the kitchen counter, where she was dividing up the chickens into portions.

"He's not," Vicky said. "I suppose he's just curious. I was surprised it's only three hundred euros to go hunting here. I'm sure it would cost a lot more in England."

She appeared to be unconscious of the tears streaming down her cheeks.

A car drew up outside the house.

"I'll go," said Pippa.

She opened the door and saw a man in a cap get out of a hatchback and walk towards her.

"*Bonsoir.* Pierre," he said, reaching out to shake her hand. His hand was moist, his face damp from sweat. She was immediately struck by his penetrating, almost hungry gaze. He had a salt-and-pepper beard and wore a striped Breton sweater under his hi-vis.

"Pippa," she said, introducing herself.

"Can I see Vicky?" he said in English, starting forward. But she stood her ground in the doorway. She had an odd feeling that he might push past her.

"She can't see you now. I'm sure you understand," she replied in French.

He stopped dead in his tracks. "Ah. Oh yes. Of course. Tell her the gendarmes are finishing up," he said. "They'll be off soon. Gilbert is taking away the boar. He'll bring round the meat for Vicky so she can distribute it."

Pippa remembered Vicky saying she had a freezer full of unwanted steaks.

"And who is Gilbert?"

"The butcher," he said.

"Oh," she said, impressed that the hunters were so well organised that they even had a butcher among them. "Maybe you could give me his phone number so we can sort that out?"

"Do you have a pen?" he asked, patting his jacket pockets. As he did so, a white van drove past. Pierre waved at the driver.

"That's Gilbert," he said.

"Would you wait here a moment?" Pippa returned to the kitchen, where Vicky was sitting where she'd left her, gently rocking.

"Who's that?" she asked.

"It's Pierre."

Vicky's eyes lit up. "Tell him I'll call him," she said, before sinking back into her reverie. Pippa found a biro on the counter and went back outside, where Pierre was wiping the sweat from his brow with the back of one hand.

"I'm sorry," he said. "We are all very upset about Alex."

He wrote down the butcher's number on the back of a store receipt and handed her the crumpled piece of paper. Pippa passed on Vicky's message.

"Did you see what happened?" she asked.

"Not really. There was a lot of noise, from the boar, of course, and then there was shouting and we all started firing

10

in that direction. I'm afraid that with several men standing only about fifty metres from each other, it's not unusual for accidents to happen." He shook his head. "Although they are not usually fatal."

CHAPTER 3

The last time Alex had made the pages of *Le Télégramme* had been only a few months earlier, when he'd led his heavy metal band in a set which had everyone rocking to the beat.

It had been a glorious summer evening on the penultimate night of the Vieilles Charrues festival. The metalheads were on their feet in the mosh pit, all in black, swaying with their phones in the air, headbanging and jumping on the grass. Alex had stripped off his torn top, the sweat dripping down his pectorals, while the crowd yelled out, "Rockface! Rockface!" in time to the hammering rhythm.

Now he was on the front page for a more distressing reason. *English rock star killed in boar hunt*, proclaimed the headline. He was sufficiently well known for the news to cross the Channel, and his death brought the tabloid press to Vicky's door in search of scandal.

"They were practically climbing up the drainpipes to get in," she told Pippa during a quiet moment in the bakery, a couple of days after the tragedy. "I had to close the curtains in the dining room to stop them peering in."

"Did you give them an interview?" Pippa enquired.

"I told them to eff off!" she exclaimed. Pippa smiled inwardly at the forceful East London accent. Nobody messed with Vicky.

"They got hold of some photos, though," Vicky went on. "Plastered all over the *Mail*. I reckon they got them from that bitch, Sharon." Sharon, Pippa knew, was Alex's first wife, with whom he had two children. Although the two women were roughly the same age, the photos she'd seen of Sharon showed her all botoxed and lip-filled — the complete opposite of Vicky.

"Or maybe from the band—"

"And the fans!" Vicky broke in. "They've been leaving flowers outside the gate. It looks like Kensington Palace when Princess Di was killed. I don't know what on earth to do with them all. And two goths managed to get over the gate and started making faces outside the bow window. They scared me half to death. My gardener had to chase them off."

"How long were you and Alex married?" Pippa asked.

"Ten years," Vicky said, and sighed. "Mind, we were shagging for ten years before that. When he was on the road, you know?"

Pippa had no response to that; it was not her world. Pippa had had a conventional and all-consuming career with an investment bank in the City, which she blamed for the break-up of her marriage. Then her dream job had come to a juddering halt. She'd won a discrimination suit against the bank, but hadn't realised until then that it meant she could never work in the industry again. Since then she'd had plenty of time to reflect on the adage "you love your job, but your job doesn't love you". So, once her daughters were at university, she'd moved to Brittany, hoping to reinvent herself. At least she was her own boss these days.

Sweeping crumbs from the stainless-steel counter, she asked Vicky about the funeral arrangements.

"I've got to get the body first, haven't I?" Vicky said. She admitted that she was thinking of moving, maybe even returning to England. "I mean, what am I going to do rattling around on my own in that dump of a château?"

"Well, I'd just say don't do anything rash," Pippa counselled. "We're here for you. In fact, why don't I make dinner for you and invite Jennifer over? Let's do it in the next few days."

She could tell that Vicky was touched by the invitation. The shock of Alex's death and her solitude in that big house must be weighing on her.

"Cool," said Vicky. "Thank you."

She picked up her bread, leaving Pippa to pull down the shutters and lock up. As she walked home, wondering about dinner, she realised she had nothing in the fridge and didn't have the energy to take the car to the supermarket. She knew bakers didn't have a life, but this was ridiculous.

As she made her way towards her front door, she glanced across the low box hedge separating her from the house next door. A Peugeot was parked there.

Two minutes later, she was knocking on her gendarme boyfriend's door holding a bottle of wine. Yann, in a smart pair of jeans, his head freshly shaven, didn't seem surprised to see her. He smiled broadly, displaying the superiority of French dentistry.

"Peeper, I was just thinking about you. Rockface, yes, that's what you called him?"

"I didn't personally, but I gather that's what his fans called him, yes," she said.

He noticed the wine and stepped forward to kiss her, twice on each cheek.

"I thought it was three times in Brittany?" she said.

"Or four," he said, giving her a hug. Why were the Bretons so inscrutable?

"Come in, come in," he said. "Have you eaten? We can dine together."

Mission accomplished. He ushered her into a kitchen identical to hers, and she drew up a chair to the table. Their cul-de-sac was a modern development of two-bedroom houses with small gardens in the centre of Louennec.

Yann prepared lamb chops, refusing her offer of help in preparing a salad to go with them. When they'd finished, Pippa fell on the ripe Brie which went perfectly with the red wine she'd brought.

She could tell from the wrapping that he'd bought the cheese from Philippe at the Saturday market in town. She leaned back in her chair, sated.

"Thank you, that was delicious," she said, pushing away her plate.

"Did you know Alex?" he asked.

"I didn't only know him, but I was there when he died!"

Yann shook his head. "Peeper, you are amazing — always at the centre of things."

She frowned slightly at the implied criticism. She trod carefully with Yann, who didn't always appreciate what he considered to be interference in investigations. But how could she help it? She couldn't stop her customers confiding in her, could she?

"Well, I happened to be there helping his wife Vicky prepare the meal for his hunting friends," she said, somewhat defensively. "It was such a shock when the accident happened."

"Accident?"

Yann shut his mouth, apparently realising that he'd already said too much.

"So, it wasn't an accident?" said Pippa. "I noticed that the report in the paper just said that he'd been killed, without saying if the death was accidental or not—"

"Precisely. For now the prosecutor isn't saying anything," said Yann. "We have to interview all the witnesses, examine the bullets, trace the gun and things like that. We need to find out who fired the fatal shot."

"Yes of course," she said. "So, it might turn out to be accidental after all?"

Yann gave a uniquely eloquent Gallic shrug that could mean everything or nothing. Then he leaned forward and kissed her.

CHAPTER 4

Jennifer stood at the kitchen sink, staring out of the window at the unkempt lawn in the back garden. Mowing the grass would have to wait for another day.

She resumed peeling the vegetables for dinner. They'd switched it from Pippa's to her place because the babysitter wasn't available that evening. Now that Jonathan was gone, childcare had become a nightmare.

Mariam had gone to stay the night with a schoolfriend in Carhaix, but at only nine, Luke couldn't be left on his own. She'd sent him off to collect the eggs from the henhouse after coming home from school, so at least she'd be ready for market the next day. She'd given him an early supper of toasted cheese, after which he'd scampered upstairs to play a video game.

She'd just finished setting the kitchen table when she heard a knock at the front door. It was exactly 8 p.m. Pippa could never get out any sooner because she only closed the bakery at seven thirty. The golden retriever, Byron, barked at the sound, but stayed where he was in his warm spot in the kitchen. At his time of life, economy of movement was everything.

"Look at your lovely daffs," said Pippa, pointing to the clusters of yellow beside the path. She had a crisp baguette in one hand. Vicky was behind her, clasping a bottle of wine. Jennifer noticed at once how gaunt she looked.

"Yes, spring is on the way, at last," Jennifer said. "Come in."

They went into the kitchen where Jennifer set down the gifts on the counter and took out a bottle of Gros Plant from the fridge.

"The usual?"

They nodded, and arranged themselves around the table.

"So, Vicky, how are you doing?" Jennifer asked after they had clinked glasses.

"I'm not. It's shit." Vicky looked as though she hadn't slept in a week. Her cheeks were cavernous and she pulled gently on a thin plait of lacklustre hair. "They're doing a post-mortem, so I can't make any decisions yet about the funeral. My life is on hold."

"What about the investigation?" Pippa asked.

"Into the accident, you mean?" Vicky asked.

Pippa nodded, keeping silent about what she'd deduced from Yann's slip-up.

"The gendarmes aren't saying anything. The others say they've all been questioned. They had to hand their guns in, apparently — for forensics, I suppose."

Pippa had completely forgotten about the boar, which was still at the butcher's. "What do you want to do about the meat from the shoot? I've got the butcher's number."

"Oh that. I've already told Gilbert to give it to the others, and to keep the rest for himself. What was I going to do with all that meat?" Vicky said.

Jennifer brought a shepherd's pie out of the oven where it had been browning. Byron watched her intently from his blanket on the floor, his head on his paws.

"It's our own minced lamb," she said. *Our.* She couldn't get used to the absence of Jonathan, who'd left home a few months earlier to live with his lover and her young daughter in town.

"What about you? How are you doing?" Vicky asked.

Jennifer waited until she'd served them the shepherd's pie and green beans before replying.

"It's hard managing on my own. Like today. I had to pluck and prepare seven broilers all by myself for market. Jonathan always helped out when he was here. Basically, I need another pair of hands on the smallholding, but I can't really afford it."

She shoved back her chair and tapped on the dishwasher. "This is the best thing I ever bought," she said. "And you know what? Unlike a human being, it never answers back."

"But you're still doing your work for the paper, are you?" Vicky asked.

"Oh yes. Between ferrying the kids to and from school. The thing is that Jonathan can't have Mariam and Luke to stay with him because Emma has a child of her own, and doesn't have room. So that means he can only see his own children at weekends during the day. It's complicated."

Her mind drifted back to the first Christmas she'd spent with just the two children and the dog. She'd had to pretend that one of the chickens was a very small turkey, since Luke had demanded turkey with all the trimmings. Mariam, now a vegan, had refused everything but sprouts and roast potatoes. They'd been reduced to watching a stupid film on Netflix because French TV was so dreadful. And Jonathan had phoned to wish them all a happy Christmas, which had upset everyone. Byron was probably the only one who'd enjoyed himself, since he was given the chicken scraps. Jennifer emerged from her reverie, realising that Vicky had asked her a question.

"Why's that?"

"Why's what?" she replied. "Oh you mean why's it complicated? Because he's working during the week, of course. Being a financial consultant, all he needs is his laptop, but he has to follow the markets," Jennifer explained. "He says he can help out in the evenings, but it never seems to happen. Like tonight, for example."

"But you're working too . . ." Vicky said.

Jennifer gave a short laugh. "Yep. Life's so unfair, isn't it?"

They tucked into their meal until Pippa broke the silence.

"It's a pity we're not doing the pantos any more. It would cheer you up. You could have joined our troupe, Vicky."

"Panto? What panto? How did we miss that last Christmas?" Vicky said.

"Probably because it never happened. Have you heard of the Louennec players?"

Vicky shook her head. "I can't say I have."

"We used to do a Christmas panto every year. Meredith's husband, Craig, was the director. Anyway, after he died we decided to revive the tradition, and Meredith wrote us a script for *Aladdin*. But then . . ." Pippa realised that she was getting into deep water. She gave a sideways glance at Jennifer, who continued.

"To cut a long story short, I was the genie in the lamp, and Jonathan was Aladdin. But after he went off with Emma, who was Princess Jasmine in the show, the whole situation became absolutely unbearable and the panto collapsed."

"Oh, I'm sorry, I had no idea," said Vicky. "Who was playing Widow Twanky?"

"Derek. He wasn't much good, frankly," said Pippa. "Although he did write himself a funny song. Anyway, it's probably just as well that we cancelled."

Jennifer smiled. "And Derek's French wife didn't have a clue about what was going on. I suspect she'd had enough of it too, especially since she was stuck with having to find the costumes."

"I'm surprised that Meredith had time for a panto, given her day job as mayor," Vicky commented.

"Wait till you hear what she wants to do now," said Jennifer. "She wants to sign up the *commune* for the annual France in Bloom competition. There's no way that can end well."

CHAPTER 5

Pippa met Jennifer a couple of days later at the Central Café, once their regular haunt after the market in Carhaix. But with Pippa now tied up at the bakery, she'd given up her stall and rarely had the time to go to town for a coffee.

She found Jennifer seated on a leatherette bench facing the street, from where they could survey the local comings and goings.

"Gwen's on her own at the bakery," Pippa said, "but I've got half an hour. I mean, I'm the boss, aren't I?"

Jennifer grinned. "So am I, but it doesn't feel like it."

"I'm worried about you," Pippa said. She reached out and squeezed her hand. "Isn't Jonathan helping out with the finances? I mean, you really do need some help, don't you?"

Jennifer looked up at the waiter, who was standing by their table. He took their order and returned to the bar, where some of the other market stallholders were relaxing over glasses of wine.

"He does contribute something, but it's not enough to cover the cost of hiring someone. My mother-in-law has offered to come and take care of the kids during the holidays. I can't say I'm mad about the idea, but that would at least free me up. April's a big planting month for me."

"I see. It doesn't sound ideal, having Jonathan's mum in the house."

"Yes, but they are her grandchildren, so it's hard to say no. It's just that she dresses like Patsy from *Ab Fab*, except worse . . ."

Pippa laughed. "Is that even possible?"

"She'd organise me to death, and I'd lose my privacy. And she's very strict with Mariam too. So, on balance . . ." Jennifer wrinkled her nose.

"That sounds like a no."

"It does, but I think I might let her come all the same," Jennifer said ruefully.

Pippa glanced over at the bar and recognised the leather jacket of Philippe, the cheesemonger from the market. She nodded in his direction.

"Talking of privacy . . . I think Philippe likes you."

Jennifer stared at her. "What makes you say that?"

"Want a bet that he'll come over? And it won't be to see me . . ."

Philippe must have sensed their eyes on him. He turned round, waved, and made his way over to them. He was tall, stockily built and his hair was receding. But he had a round, smiling face that made him one of the most popular stallholders.

"*Bonjour*, Jennifer, *salut*, Peeper. How were your takings today?"

"Good," Jennifer said. "I sold everything, and only have two chickens left for private customers. In fact, I might drop one off for Vicky at the château."

"The château? Is she the wife of Rockface? Everyone's talking about this," he said. He shook his head. "Very sad. But it's not surprising that accidents happen. The boars are bigger and bigger, and all the hunters shoot at once. And there are more *sangliers* every year. I read in the paper that this month almost three thousand were killed. They said it was hundreds more than a year ago, and that's only in Finistère!"

He gestured animatedly as he spoke.

21

"It's a wonder there aren't more accidents, then," said Jennifer.

Philippe glanced back towards his friends at the bar.

"*J'arrive*," he called out.

"I must go," he said to Jennifer. "See you next week."

When he had gone, Pippa smiled broadly. "See. I said he's soft on you. You're about the same age . . ."

Jennifer blushed. "Don't be silly."

"By the way, Yann says they don't know whether it was an accident or not."

"You mean it could have been murder? But that's ridiculous. Why would anyone want to kill Alex?" Jennifer said.

"I'm just saying what he told me. Have you heard anything from any of your customers?"

"No. But then I've had other things on my mind. Have you?" Jennifer said.

"Well one of the hunters is Jean-Michel, from the council," Pippa said. "He's one of my regulars. He brought the hounds for the *battue* and he says it was absolute chaos — the boar was wounded and was chasing one of the other hunters, which caused them all to start firing. I mean, those things can weigh two hundred kilos. The men must have feared for their lives."

"That still sounds like an accident to me," said Jennifer. "I'm lucky the paper didn't call me in on that story, what with being friends with Vicky and everything."

"Yes. It struck me that she seemed to be more than friendly with Pierre, one of the hunters, but there might be nothing in it. As for Philippe . . . does he know about you and Jonathan splitting up?"

"How would I know?" Jennifer began picking up her things and gestured at the waiter for the bill. Smiling, she wagged a finger at her friend. "Now look you. Just because my husband left me for a younger model doesn't mean I need a boyfriend."

Pippa grinned. "Why not? Nobody would blame you. You need a helper on the farm, don't you?"

CHAPTER 6

Despite having been elected mayor almost a year earlier, Meredith's stomach still churned with anxiety whenever she had to chair a council meeting.

She was the last to arrive, and sat down awkwardly with one leg sideways as she was periodically afflicted with gout. The fourteen councillors from Louennec and the surrounding rural area had already taken their places around the long oval table in the *mairie*, and her two deputies were seated beside her.

Jean-Michel was responsible for the environment and agriculture. As usual, he was wearing a suit, having come straight from his job as a freight company manager. The other deputy mayor, Christine, was a retired accountant in charge of finance and social outreach. And at the far end of the table sat the *secrétaire de la mairie*, Sylvie Le Goff, her ramrod-straight back signalling to the assembled councillors that she was the one in charge.

"Welcome everybody," said Meredith. "Nobody missing? Sylvie?" Mme Le Goff gave a barely perceptible shake of her head. "Right. Let's get straight down to business."

Craig had told her that when he was a councillor, the mayor had always gone round the table, shaking hands and kissing the women on the cheek in the traditional *bise*. But

Meredith had decided to dispense with this time-consuming convention; after all, how could she ever give the horrible Sylvie a kiss? Following approval of the minutes of the last meeting, point one of the agenda was Meredith's proposal that the village take part in the France in Bloom competition.

Sylvie cleared her throat. Everyone knew she was about to complain, because she always did.

"I would just like to say something," she said, with a tight-lipped smile. "This point on the agenda is already being talked about in the village. That shouldn't happen. First the council adopts a position, and *then* we inform the *commune*."

"Yes," said Meredith. "I'm sorry. I may have mentioned it to one or two people."

Sylvie frowned but said nothing more.

"Anyway," Meredith went on, "the point is that we've never taken part in this competition before, and if we're interested, we need to apply before the end of the month, so there's no time to lose. Are we all agreed that we should participate? It means we're going to have to encourage as many people as possible to join in."

Armel, a local dairy farmer, raised his hand. He and Meredith hadn't seen eye to eye after he'd agreed to a sub-station on his land for an onshore wind farm project that had divided the villagers. From his perspective, the countryside was a working enterprise, and putting flowers around the village was an unnecessary luxury. "What about the second homes?" he asked. "Those people aren't here often enough to take care of their gardens—"

"That's not true," someone retorted.

A third person wanted to know whether the villagers could expect their landscaping efforts to be subsidised.

"Don't you think it would be sufficient reward to win our first star?" said Meredith. "That would be great for a first attempt."

She took a few minutes to explain the procedure for entering the competition. "It costs less than a hundred euros to apply," she noted, "which is nothing." The *commune* would

24

contact the Finistère department with a pitch explaining why they wanted to become one of the Villes et Villages Fleuris. If the departmental authorities agreed that the application had potential, they had until September to send off the final project proposal to the regional committee, which would then make its decision.

"And the regional authorities would let us know in October or November," Meredith continued. "But the first hurdle is to persuade the people in Quimper that we're serious. Once that happens, they will provide technical help and advice as we go along."

"What about four stars?" somebody asked.

Sylvie pursed her lips. "That's for the national jury to decide. The first three are handed out by the region."

"Let's not get ahead of ourselves," Meredith said. "Frankly, I'd be happy with one star this first time. There are clear advantages — for example, attracting tourists who would spend time in the village, thereby boosting our local businesses.

"It's important that we all realise that this isn't just about flowers, but about promoting our village in all sorts of ways. The judges won't just be horticulturalists; they'll be specialists in tourism and the environment. It will be a challenge. But I'm sure we'll be up to the task."

After a few more minutes of grumbling around the table, Meredith called a vote. To her surprise, only two councillors objected — Armel, and a retired teacher who argued that it would represent too much work because she doubted that people would want to keep up the effort for three years.

When somebody asked why three years, she said, "Because once we've obtained a first star, we're on the ladder and are inspected every three years."

Meredith turned to Jean-Michel. "I think putting together the application is your job," she said. "But it's the duty of every one of us to promote the idea among the villagers. So do pass any suggestions you may have to Jean-Michel here."

They moved down the agenda, approving a request from a local association to hold a *fest-noz* of traditional dancing in the *salle des fêtes* the following month. Again, there were complaints. A couple of the older councillors recalled that in the old days, the *fest-noz* had become an excuse for a get-together involving copious amounts of alcohol.

"These days, it's like a dancing class, it's not so much fun," said one.

"Yes, but at least you learn something, rather than just getting drunk," Christine chipped in. "And the weather might be nice in May, so we'll have a good turnout."

"Any other items?" Meredith asked. For once there were none. But Meredith could tell from her pursed lips that Madame le Goff had her own thoughts about the flower initiative.

CHAPTER 7

Jennifer made out her mother-in-law the minute she descended from the train. Why was she wearing stilettos with her knock-off Chanel jacket and jeans for a stay in the French countryside? Surely she was aware that Jennifer was up to her knees in muck most of the time?

A young man got down behind Prue, carrying her suitcase. Jennifer waited for her at the station entrance.

Prue emerged, and started rummaging in her handbag. Jennifer, fearing that she was about to pay her long-suffering helper for his trouble, said, "Here, let me take that," and seized the suitcase handle. The young man clearly couldn't get away fast enough.

It took two of them to heave the case into the car boot. What on earth had she put in it?

"I've brought some gifts for the children," Prue explained, evidently noticing Jennifer's reaction.

They had to pick up the children on the way home. First, Mariam, who was waiting by the school gate with her friend, Pervenche. They were bent over a phone and Jennifer had to sound the horn to get their attention.

Mariam waved off her friend. Her face grew taut when she saw Prue in the passenger seat.

"Hello, Granny Prue." She got in the back and took out her phone.

"Hello, Mariam. You can look up from the phone, you know, when you've got a visitor. Have you lost weight, dear?" she asked.

"No," said Mariam, returning her attention to the phone.

Jennifer had hoped that having Prue for the Easter holidays would give her the space to pick up the pace on the smallholding. What she didn't want was to have to negotiate peace between a warring thirteen-year-old and her fifty-seven-year-old granny.

"We'll just pick up Luke and then be off home," she said brightly.

"You're quite a way from the nearest town, aren't you? I checked the address on the internet," said Prue.

"Carhaix is actually only five kilometres, although it's a bit far to walk," said Jennifer. "And the house is a fair way from Louennec, the nearest village. One of my friends runs the bakery there, which is convenient. You might get to meet her while you're here."

"And of course I'll be seeing Jonathan as well. They live in town, I understand," said Prue. She pulled down the passenger mirror and examined her make-up. Pursing her lips, she took out her lipstick and applied it liberally.

Jennifer drove on in silence until they reached Louennec. Luke waved to them from the pavement outside the school.

"You're late," he complained.

"Look who's here — Granny Prue," Jennifer said. "I had to wait for her train at the station, that's what held us up."

He joined Mariam in the back. In the rear-view mirror, Jennifer saw them exchange a complicit glance.

Luke kept the conversation going until they reached home, pointing out such local attractions as a roadside shrine to a car crash victim, a bird's nest here, roadkill there.

"Mummy, can we show Granny Prue the alpacas?" he asked.

"Not today, darling. We'll go straight home now."

At the pig farm she turned down the lane towards their wooded dell.

"Do you want to see the animals?" Luke asked Prue as soon as Jennifer pulled up beside the house. She saw the house with Prue's eyes: the white stucco starting to look the worse for wear under the slate roof tinged with yellow lichen. Some sad-looking potted plants clung to the ground-floor granite windowsills. A gnarled wisteria was draped untidily around the front door, bristling with buds.

"Let's do that later, shall we?" Jennifer said. "Granny's had a long journey from London. She must be tired."

"I'll show you your room and make us a cup of tea," she said to Prue. The two women dragged Prue's suitcase out of the car and along the path to the front door, where Byron was waiting for them, tail wagging. The children escaped upstairs, their duty done, Luke apparently having forgotten about the "special" present his grandmother had told him she'd brought.

"Well!" Prue stood in the hall. Jennifer, trying to follow her gaze, wasn't certain what she was referring to, but Prue began patting the dog. "Do you think Byron remembers me from London?"

"I'm sure he does," Jennifer said.

"That's the trouble with golden retrievers, they get fat with age."

"He's arthritic, actually," Jennifer said, "so he doesn't move around too much these days." As though on cue, Byron sank heavily to the floor. Jennifer left the suitcase by the door and led the way into the living/dining room. Prue scanned the furniture forensically and opted for the sofa, flopping down and kicking off her shoes. Her toenails were painted scarlet.

"Ah, that feels good."

"I'll put the kettle on," said Jennifer, heading into the kitchen. She'd repainted it since Jonathan's departure, in an attempt to cheer herself up. The scuffed white paint had been replaced by duck-egg blue. She'd had to take down Luke's drawings from school and had replaced them with a board on which she'd stuck a selection of family photos. Her next task would be to replace the old wooden cupboards. "No need to get up."

"But I'm here to help you," Prue called out, stretching her legs and waggling her painted toes.

A few minutes later, Jennifer reappeared with two mugs of tea and biscuits on a tray.

Prue leaned forward and lowered her voice to a whisper. "So, tell me, how are you managing without Jonathan? Any chance of a reconciliation?"

Jennifer immediately regretted having invited her mother-in-law to spend a week on the smallholding. Nevertheless, she owed her the truth.

"I don't think so. I'm still pretty angry." About to tell her of his lying and deception, she remembered that Prue was Jonathan's mother, and stopped herself in time. "We've not quite worked out the childcare yet. You see, Luke and Mariam can't spend the night at Emma's because she has a daughter, and they just don't have room."

"Yes. I heard. By the way, how *is* Mariam?"

Jennifer wondered how much Prue had heard from Jonathan. She presumed she knew about Mariam having been bullied at school last year. Before she had time to reply, Prue said, "I mean, how is she fitting in? What with being adopted and all that."

"You mean because she's a different colour from the other pupils? Actually, she's fitting in well, and she's made friends." Jennifer hadn't intended to be sharp, but she resented the implicit racism of the question; Prue was obviously referring to Mariam's Somali background. "You'll see for yourself, anyway. She's a normal thirteen-year-old, with all the usual adolescent turmoil."

"Has she got a boyfriend?"

"At that age? I don't think so!" Jennifer spluttered. She stood up. "Let me take your suitcase upstairs and I'll show you your room so you can unpack and relax. There's only one bathroom, I'm afraid, but there's a downstairs loo as well."

She manhandled the case up the oak staircase, humping it round the corner to the landing, while Prue followed behind. With a feeling of relief she left her mother-in-law to her unpacking.

Downstairs again, Jennifer busied herself peeling and slicing vegetables for dinner. About half an hour later, Luke came into the kitchen in his wellies.

"Where are you going in those?" Jennifer asked. "I thought I told you to leave them in the hall."

"Yes, but I'm going to show Granny Prue the animals."

With a sigh, Jennifer put down the knife. "I'll come with you." Prue was on her way downstairs wearing jeans, a denim jacket over a pullover, and a pair of shoes that she no doubt considered "sensible" but which wouldn't survive five minutes in the country mud.

"You'd better borrow a pair of these," Jennifer said, pointing to the collection of rubber boots in the hall.

Equipped with suitable footwear, the three of them set out, followed at a distance by Byron. Luke picked up a discarded branch from the ground to use as a walking stick.

"Shall we show her the pond, Mummy?" he asked.

They walked along a grassy track to the furthest point of the smallholding where the fishpond was located. Behind it was the vegetable patch and a plastic-covered greenhouse for the tomato plants.

"Why have you got wire netting over the pond?" Prue enquired.

"Daddy put it on because the heron was eating the goldfish!" Luke said.

"You've got goldfish in there? I can't see anything but pondweed."

"Yes, there are about a dozen," said Jennifer. "Would you like to see the sheep?"

She led the way to the sheep pasture, where Rambo the ram was chewing a mouthful of hay, and another sheep was ambling towards them.

"That's Blackie. She's pregnant!" Luke told Prue as he hung over the gate. Prue's expression, however, said she was less than impressed by all the marvels Luke was proudly showing her.

"She's expecting two lambs, actually," said Jennifer. *Another vet's bill.*

Prue looked up at the sky. "Is it going to rain? Perhaps we'd better go in."

Luke showed her the rabbit hutches on the way back. "This one's Lady Gaga," he said, referring to the mother rabbit, which had soft white fur. Animated at last, Prue cooed over the baby rabbits.

Closer to the house, they passed the two chicken runs.

"These are the broilers," Jennifer said, pointing towards the one further up the slope.

"Broilers?"

"Yes. We raise them for their meat. They're the ones I sell on the market. The others are down there," she gestured towards the second enclosure, "where we keep the laying hens."

"I see," said Prue. "It must be a lot of work, taking care of all of them."

"Yes, it is," said Jennifer. *Isn't that why you're here — to help out?*

"That's where Mariam opened the gate to the chicken run and they all got out!" Luke exclaimed excitedly, pointing towards the layers. "We had to go looking for them."

Jennifer had hoped that Jonathan wouldn't have mentioned the incident, which dated from Mariam's troubled period at school, but Prue nodded as though she knew the story. They'd lost six chickens that night. Maybe that's what had prompted Prue's questions about Mariam.

"Come on, let's go back in," she said. The three of them trailed back to the house.

At the gate, Jennifer remembered to check the post and found the daily newspaper in the mailbox.

The front page headline jumped out at her: *Rockface: was it murder?*

CHAPTER 8

Pippa folded her white cotton apron, locked up the bakery for the night and lowered the metal shutters.

She walked past the *mairie* on her way home, and noticed a hanging basket of pink petunias on a lamp post outside the building. It hadn't been there before and she smiled, guessing it to be part of Meredith's campaign to take part in the France in Bloom competition.

Turning into her street, she was surprised to see that the flowerbed belonging to the house on the corner had been turned upside down. Had they been gardening too enthusiastically over the weekend? Or had it been destroyed by wild animals, maybe a family of boar? She remembered having noticed neat rows of bedding plants only a few days ago. She'd have to ask the couple who lived there about it; the wife was one of her regulars.

As she was unlocking her front door, she heard the phone ringing. It was Vicky.

"What's up?" Pippa asked.

"Have you seen the paper?"

"No, why?"

"It's disgraceful! My phone hasn't stopped ringing all day. It basically says — without a shred of evidence — that

I'm having an affair and that I plotted with my lover to knock off Alex!"

"Oh? So where do they get that idea from?" Pippa said.

"'Anonymous sources', of course," Vicky said sardonically. "Somebody must have seen me and Pierre in Carhaix together and made up a story about it."

"Pierre? Not the guy who was at the boar hunt?" Pippa said.

"Yes. Why?"

Just as she had suspected. "I had wondered whether there might be something going on between you, but I thought it was none of my business."

"Right, but to jump to the conclusion that I wanted to kill Alex, that's absolutely fucking outrageous! I'm going to sue those bastards."

"Hold on, hold on. Does that mean they've done the ballistics test? If they can identify the gun that fired the fatal bullet, or bullets, then they can presumably trace the murderer."

"I know, Pippa. But the story doesn't say anything about the investigation. And I told the gendarmes where they could get off when they asked me about my relationship with Pierre. In fact, they've barely contacted me at all since I went in to identify Alex. I only know that their 'criminal research institute', or whatever it's called, is doing the forensics. You know what I think?"

Pippa waited.

"I reckon they don't give a shit because it was a boar hunt on private property. They're just assuming it was an accident. This mad theory about me and Pierre is going to muddy the waters, though, isn't it?"

"Look, I've no idea. I can have a word with Yann if you like, although the investigators are based in Brest, so I'm not sure how much he knows about it. It certainly sounds like the paper has gone out on a limb with this story."

"You're not kidding!"

Pippa repressed a sigh. She was tired and hungry. "Leave this with me. But I won't have time to do anything tonight. I've just got home."

"Of course. Sorry."

"Let's get together soon. OK?"

"OK. Great. Thanks."

Vicky rang off. Pippa poured herself a glass of Gros Plant and sat at the kitchen table. She should ask Yann, but she hadn't noticed his car in the drive. She got up and peered through her front window. The car definitely wasn't there. She returned to the kitchen and munched thoughtfully on a homemade cheese straw.

She rang Jennifer, and was about to give up when she answered, her voice almost a whisper. What was the matter with everyone tonight?

"Jennifer? What's wrong?"

"Hang on a sec." Pippa heard the sound of furniture scraping on the floor, and then Jennifer was back on the line.

"My mother-in-law's here, so I can't talk. We're just finishing dinner, sorry."

"Of course. I'd completely forgotten. How's it going?" Pippa said.

"Oh, just fabulous!"

Pippa burst out laughing. "I can imagine."

"At the moment, Prue is trying to persuade Mariam to eat a lamb chop. You can imagine how that's going because a while back, Mariam decided to become a vegan."

Pippa smiled. "I was actually ringing about Vicky. She's furious about the article in the paper — you've seen it, haven't you? About her and a boyfriend plotting to kill Alex. Allegedly. She's threatening to sue. I told you I thought she was having it off with that guy Pierre, and it turns out she is."

"According to the paper, at least."

"Yes, but it's a completely different thing to then suggest that she might have got him to shoot Alex, isn't it?" Pippa said.

"That's what I thought too when I read it. But the whole story was based on anonymous sources. Somebody must have an axe to grind with Pierre, or Vicky, or both, don't you think?" said Jennifer.

"Could be," said Pippa. "You know what they're like round here. But what if the pair of them did do it?"

CHAPTER 9

Vicky mounted the spiral staircase leading up to the study. Above, the scraping of the handyman's trowel was almost drowned out by loud music.

"*Attention*," she said, squeezing past him. As he stood up to let her go by, she caught sight of the claws of a bird tattooed at the base of his spine. The music was still playing, he hadn't bothered to turn it off. She recognised the song as one of Alex's.

"Everything OK, Tanguy?" she asked in her rudimentary French, almost shouting over the noise.

"*Oui, madame*." She couldn't help staring at his stainless-steel nose ring. Vicky had sported a tongue stud when she was on the road with Alex, but had taken it out for good after it had got infected. She'd always enjoyed people's reactions when she'd opened her mouth to speak — they couldn't take their eyes off it. It sat there, framed by her black-painted lips, like a pearl in an oyster. But the fun had worn off with the infection. It was all very well suffering for beauty, but that was ridiculous.

Tanguy gestured towards the smooth, freshly plastered surface covering a hole in the corner of the stone staircase, waiting for her to admire his workmanship.

"*Très bien*," she said, screwing up her eyes, and carried on past him up the ill-lit stairs.

The study was at the very top of the restored turret, above the master bedroom. Vicky wondered if she'd ever get the east turret fixed, now that Alex had gone. Maybe she should consult Tanguy about getting an estimate from a local builder. But that could wait.

With Alex gone, the château, with all its nooks and crannies, had begun to give her the creeps. It was, without doubt, too big for one person, yet she never seemed to have any privacy. At every turn, one of her staff would emerge from the shadows, with a "*Bonjour, madame*" that made her jump.

She reached the study and paused in the doorway, panting from the climb up the stairs. The circular room had only a single small window, so she switched on the light, and was confronted by a mass of paper. Receipts and invoices and who knew what other documents lay strewn on and around Alex's desk. Her husband had been a technophobe who had insisted on conducting every transaction on paper. If she was lucky, he'd pass them to her for action. Now, she dreaded having to sort through this mess; every scrap of paper had the potential to reveal an unpleasant surprise.

Her own desk was a model of tidiness: all her documents were in files in the computer that sat on its clean surface. She sat down in front of her screen and consulted the payroll. The other staff were paid at the end of each month, but Tanguy was off the books, and, for some reason known only to Alex, was paid five hundred euros in cash every two weeks. It was too late now to do anything about what she considered a far too generous arrangement, unless she got rid of him. He certainly hadn't been to charm school. But she had to admit that the man had his uses.

She spent a few minutes checking her files before shutting down the computer. Then she opened the top drawer of the heavy oak desk and opened a safe box from which she took out ten fifty-euro notes. She slid the money into a plain white envelope and wrote TANGUY on the front, as usual.

Vicky wished she'd brought a cup of tea with her, but couldn't face going back downstairs to put the kettle on. She sighed, stood up, and moved across to Alex's desk, where she flexed her fingers and placed a hand on an unsteady pile of papers. Where to start?

She opened the top drawer, which was filled with spare keys. Each one was labelled in Alex's spidery handwriting. The next drawer down contained family photos, some loose and others still in the packets from the shop. She took a few of them out, put them on the desk, and lost track of time, flooded with memories of Alex's gigs and their rockers' wedding. Recent photos of their life since they'd moved to Brittany were mixed up with snaps of Sharon and Alex's children, all of them in various states of undress.

Vicky was studying a twenty-year-old photo of Alex, with long hair and a pair of outsize glasses, when she heard voices on the staircase. Quickly, she shoved the pictures back in the drawer.

She recognised Pierre's voice and realised he must have let himself in. Maybe they should have been more discreet about their relationship. It was just the sort of thing to set tongues in the village wagging, culminating in that outrageous newspaper article. She couldn't make out what Pierre and Tanguy were discussing, but they certainly sounded animated.

She picked up the envelope and switched off the light before making her way down to the two men. She handed the envelope to Tanguy, who took it without a word, before greeting Pierre. The two of them went down the steps, Pierre in the lead just in case she fell.

When they reached the kitchen, she asked him what he and Tanguy had been talking about.

"*Rien de particulier*," he said. Nothing special. His dismissive reply annoyed her.

"Come on, tell me."

Pierre shrugged. "Oh, just politics."

In Vicky's short experience of France, everyone was obsessed with politics. Or the local gossip, especially in the case of Bleuzenn, her cook.

"In fact, we were talking about your friend the mayor, Marie," he said.

"Meredith," she corrected him. "What's the problem with her?"

"She wants to shake things up in the village, but it's not going to work. I mean, we're farmers round here, not landscape architects." Laughing at his own wit, he pulled her towards him. Vicky had succumbed to an animal attraction for Pierre, cheating on Alex for the first time, despite the risk of being found out. She was still surprised that she should have fallen so passionately for a dour Frenchman with the calloused hands of a farmer. He enfolded her in an embrace, burying his head in a cloud of orange hair. His beard tickled her cheek.

"I don't want my field to be turned into a garden just to get a star in some stupid competition," he whispered in her ear. "And we don't like being pushed around by foreigners either — that's what Tanguy says."

CHAPTER 10

Jennifer stomped around the kitchen, preparing the children's breakfast, before loading up the car with her market produce.

Prue was nowhere to be seen. Instead of lightening Jennifer's load, she'd become an additional burden. She was rarely seen before mid-morning, and when she did come downstairs, she expected to be served. So much for helping out with the children.

She'd even managed to drive a wedge between them, giving Luke, with much song and dance, a 3D puzzle of Hogwarts Castle, while Mariam got a cheap beaded necklace and matching bracelet.

So, Jennifer was somewhat taken aback when Prue made a dramatic entrance at seven forty-five. She wore a silk dressing gown and heeled slippers as though arriving at an awards ceremony, just as Jennifer was about to leave.

"Be careful on the stairs in those heels," Jennifer called out. "We wouldn't want you to trip and fall over."

"One sleeps so well here in the country, don't you find?" said Prue. "Are you off to the Saturday market? You see, I did remember."

"Yes, I am. Mariam, can you make breakfast for Granny Prue?" Mariam threw her a dark look but got up to pour Prue some coffee.

"Thank you, dear," she said. "I'll just have one of these." She helped herself to a croissant. "You do know I'm invited to Jonathan's for dinner tonight, don't you?"

It was the first Jennifer had heard about it, but was relieved that they'd have the house to themselves for a change.

"And I've been invited by Pervenche," said Mariam.

"Right, so it looks like it's you and me, Luke."

"Can Alain come over? He's got a new game."

"Oh. All right." Jennifer was running late. She'd already fed the rabbits and shredded a bale of hay for the sheep, who came running out of their shed, baaing loudly, pushing each other out of the way. On her way back to the house, she'd gone up to feed the broilers. The henhouse had been her last stop. She'd dropped food waste into the chicken run before letting the chickens out of the coop, where the cock was always the first to push his way out. Typical male. Inside the run, she'd poured out their water and felt inside the nesting boxes. Her reward was six eggs that she'd popped in her pocket.

Jennifer put on her jacket and said over her shoulder, "I'll be back at lunchtime." *But don't put yourselves out.*

She was the last stallholder to arrive, and she set out her organic veggies, flowers and eggs in a hurry, taking care not to break any of the eggs.

Her first customer was Derek, dressed in his running gear and carrying a canvas tote bag under his arm.

"Morning, Jennifer!" he called out cheerily. She hadn't seen him since Alex's death, and immediately asked him whether he'd read the latest article in the paper.

"It's gossip, if you ask me," he said. "I didn't know about Vicky having a lover, but if she did, so what? It's not a crime, is it? I'll take half a dozen eggs, please. No chickens this week?"

"Next time," she said, and lowered her voice. "Maybe somebody's got it in for Vicky and Pierre, leaking it to the press like that." She said no more, but the newspaper article had had its effect. Like a worm in her brain, it had changed her attitude towards Vicky. Could she be capable of murder? A crime of passion? Pushing the thought aside, she packed Derek's eggs into a cardboard container, and asked him if he needed anything else. He picked up a bunch of fresh mint, sniffing its leaves.

"I heard that you were a guest at the hunt," she said, holding out her machine for him to tap his card. Few people came to the market with cash these days, and the younger customers used their phones for everything. "Does that mean you weren't actually shooting?"

"That's right, I wasn't," he said. "They had this wooden viewing stand at the edge of the wood so I could see what was going on. Except that I didn't. I just heard a commotion, shots being fired and then shouts, so I thought I'd better go and see if anyone had been hurt. That's when I found Alex on the ground, poor man."

"Was he on his own?" Jennifer asked. "What about the others? Where were they?"

"They came running up when they realised something had happened. A couple of boars were barging around as well, which was quite frightening."

"What about Pierre? Do you think he was the one who fired the fatal shot? Even if it was an accident?"

"Honestly, Jennifer, I've no idea. It was impossible to tell. I did see everyone stowing their guns in their vehicles afterwards but they had to take them out again for the gendarmes. I suppose the ballistics guys will be able to link the bullets to the gun and its owner."

"Well he didn't shoot himself in the bottom, did he? Somebody must have had a grudge against Alex. Was it Gilbert the butcher? I use him sometimes to slaughter my rabbits. He seems perfectly nice to me. And what about Armel, the dairy farmer?"

"I'd never met him before, although he and Jean-Michel are both on the council aren't they, so I presume they're upstanding members of the community. As for Pascal, the other farmer — a pig farmer, I believe — I'd never met him before either, but he seemed perfectly charming. Anyway, I'm sure the police are doing their job."

She shrugged. "Or maybe we'll never know. Give my regards to Solenn . . . I've not seen her at the market for a while."

"She only gets out her stall in the tourist season," he said. "The locals don't buy much jewellery, even the Breton kind. And it's only a hobby. Don't forget she's still got a day job," Derek said. His wife worked as a dentist's receptionist in Carhaix.

"Look, why don't you come over for drinks and nibbles?" Jennifer said, on impulse. "I could round up the others. It'd be just like the old days, when we were doing the panto."

"That would be great. Let's do it. Just tell us when." He moved off, just as a small queue was forming behind him. Jennifer watched him head towards the cheese stall and realised that Philippe was looking in their direction. She gave him a wave and he gestured with his thumb in the direction of the Central Café.

She nodded and smiled before she'd even had time to think, then busied herself by selecting a bunch of red peonies for her next customer.

* * *

Jennifer packed up her things and headed for the café, spotting Philippe standing at the bar with his friend Jean-Luc, who had a popular crêpe stall at the market. She remembered how paranoid Pippa had been about the competition he represented when she was struggling to sell her homemade curry to the Bretons while doing her bakery diploma. Now the situation was reversed, and Pippa was the one earning more. Jean-Luc was noticeably broad-shouldered with ripped arms that seemed incongruous in a crêpe-seller — Jennifer had heard that he was a former Olympic rower. He'd fallen in love with a woman from Carhaix and moved from the coast to be with her, but almost as soon as he arrived, she'd dumped him. Jennifer respected him for staying and making a new life in the town, minus the girlfriend. Some Bretons seemed to have the sea in their soul.

Philippe made space for Jennifer at the bar between himself and Jean-Luc, who was sipping a *ballon de rouge*.

"A glass of wine?" Philippe asked.

"Just a *café noisette*, thanks," she said. "Good day?"

"Not bad," he said. "But I get the impression people are cutting back because of the economic climate. And the youngsters don't buy much cheese. They're all vegans now, aren't they?"

"They are," she said. "Like my daughter. Her favourite dish used to be mac and cheese, but she won't touch it now."

"Mac and cheese?" he asked. "You mean there's another English gastronomic dish besides *rosbif*?"

Jennifer laughed. "It's basically macaroni with a cheese sauce." Philippe rolled his eyes at Jean-Luc. Obviously, a Breton would never be seen dead eating such a thing.

"I read the story in the paper about Rockface," he said, drawing down his lips and nodding slowly as if to say, *it's a bad business*.

"Yes. I didn't know about Pierre and Vicky. Did you?" she asked.

"No. Jean-Luc?" His friend shrugged. Apparently he wasn't *au courant* either.

"What does Pierre do for a living?" she asked.

"Did you know Didier? He had a field where he grew hemp. After he died, his wife needed money and Pierre bought the land as well as a field next to it. I think he even bought the rope machine that had belonged to Didier's father."

"Ah," Jennifer replied. "I get it. That's how he would have met Alex and Vicky. The rope thing. He probably helped out with Alex's shows."

With a "*Salut*" to them both, Jean-Luc swallowed the last of his red wine and turned to go, leaving some small change on the bar for the waiter.

There was a brief silence, and then Philippe said, "I heard that your husband is in Carhaix now. Do you need

45

any help on the farm? If you do, I'm free this afternoon. It must be hard for you now, with all the planting."

"I, er, thank you. Yes, it is a busy time." She gave him a grateful smile and was about to accept when she remembered Prue. "But I'm afraid my mother-in-law is here at the moment, looking after the children, so I don't think you could come then."

She didn't know why she'd said that. What harm would there be if he came to give a hand on the plot? "At least she's *supposed* to be looking after the children," she added, "but in fact she's creating even more work for me."

"Ah. Mothers-in-law. I used to have one too. But me, when I divorced my wife, I also lost the mother-in-law so I was twice lucky!"

"And do you have children?"

"A girl, yes. She's fourteen, and mostly stays with her mother in Rennes."

"Your daughter is just a year older than mine, then. We adopted her when she was a baby, and she had a few difficulties settling in here, because she looks different."

He nodded sympathetically. "Yes, I've seen her with you. Where is she from?"

"Somalia, originally. Her mother abandoned her in a refugee camp in Kenya when she was only a few months old. It's a sad story."

"But you gave her advantages that she'd never have had otherwise," said Philippe.

"That's what Jonathan used to say. And our son, Luke, he's nine. Completely different from Mariam."

She took out her phone to check the time. "That reminds me, I'd better go. I told them I'd be back in time for lunch, and I don't know whether my mother-in-law will have prepared anything."

She got out her wallet to pay for her coffee but Philippe placed his hand on hers. She almost jumped at the touch.

"If you don't need me this afternoon, what about this evening?" he asked.

Why not? "I'd like that," she said. "Luke will be in, but he'll be upstairs with a friend. And my mother-in-law will be out at Jonathan's. If you want, you could come over for a drink or something once I've taken Mariam to her friend's in Carhaix."

CHAPTER 11

Pippa watched through the shop window as Jean-Michel parked his SUV outside the *mairie* and crossed the road to the bakery.

It was 6.30 p.m. Jean-Michel came in every day at the same time, either on his way home from work or leaving the *mairie*, so she always left his slightly undercooked — *pas trop cuite* — baguette on one side for him. He seemed out of sorts this afternoon, which wasn't like him.

"*Bonsoir*," she said. "*Tout va bien?*"

He harrumphed. "The villagers are revolting over the Villes et Villages Fleuris," he said, "and it's my job to promote the idea of us joining the programme."

"I noticed the hanging basket outside the *mairie*. Very nice," she said.

"Did you see the poster too? We're getting flyers ready to distribute to everyone," he said. "I've only got a few more days before the application deadline."

"But what's the problem?" she asked. "I don't see why anybody would object to prettifying the *commune*."

"Some villagers feel the programme is being shoved down their throats. They say they've got enough work as it is, without being under pressure to tidy up their gardens and spend money on flowers.

"*Pff,*" he added, scornfully. He took out his card to pay, and Pippa handed over the baguette.

"One of my neighbours' flowerbeds is a mess," said Pippa. "I noticed that all the soil in the front garden had been turned over, and the flowers were gone. I wondered whether they were getting ready for the challenge, or if some animal had dug it up."

"*Ils ont tout saccagé!*" he exclaimed. "We don't know who's responsible, but on the same night several villagers had their freshly planted flowerbeds uprooted and destroyed! Your neighbours complained about what happened to them."

"You mean it was deliberate sabotage?"

"Of course, my dear Peeper. You don't know what the French are capable of; they always react with violence when they disagree with something. And unfortunately, it's getting worse because mayors are increasingly becoming a target of their anger and frustration."

"Oh dear. I'm sorry to hear that. Getting *ville fleurie* status seems like a good idea to me. I'm planning to improve my garden for the challenge, if it's any consolation. I feel motivated."

"Sometimes I wonder if it's worth it. But Meredith wants us to go ahead, and it would be good for the village." Jean-Michel lowered his voice. "May I speak *entre nous*?"

"Of course," she replied.

"I wouldn't be surprised if it's not Sylvie Le Goff who's behind it."

"You mean the *secrétaire de la mairie*? Nothing would surprise me where that woman's concerned," said Pippa. "And she doesn't like Meredith, does she?"

About to respond, Jean-Michel shut his lips. Another customer had come in. At the same moment, Gwen came in from the back looking for something, her hands covered with flour.

"So we'll see," he said. "*Bonne soirée*, Peeper."

* * *

Pippa returned home just as dusk was falling. In the sun's last rays she saw that her neighbours had put in some bedding plants to replace those that had been pulled up. She wondered how long they would last. What if the flower terrorists returned and pulled them up again? *Who would do such a thing?*

Inside the house, she Facetimed her elder daughter, who was camping in the Lake District with her boyfriend. She'd been hoping they would come to Brittany for Easter, and was now banking on a visit in the summer during the long vacation.

"Hi, Mum!" Joanne had to shout to make herself heard over the roar of the wind.

"Where on earth are you?" Pippa asked.

She understood that, at the third attempt, the pair of them had hiked up Latrigg Fell. "Look at the view from here — it's amazing," Joanne said, turning the phone round so that Pippa could see Keswick huddled below and the dark waters of Derwentwater beyond. But Joanne's anorak was flapping so much in the wind that they ended the conversation with a promise to talk again soon.

Pippa pottered around in the kitchen for a while, preparing some salad. Suddenly she remembered her promise to Vicky that she'd mention her concerns about the newspaper allegations to Yann. She moved to her living-room window and saw his Peugeot parked in the drive.

She stepped outside. The light in his sitting room was on. She knew he liked to relax after work by listening to music with his headphones on, but she rang the doorbell anyway. He opened the door with a smile, the hall light making his shaven head gleam.

"Are you coming in?" he asked.

"Not just now, Yann. We're still seeing each other on Monday, aren't we?" Monday was Pippa's day off, but Yann was on a rota which made planning anything in advance difficult.

He nodded. "Of course. On Saturday we'll be busy, because we heard the youths will be out again on their motorbikes."

"Another urban rodeo? Oh no! All that noise."

"Not here. In Carhaix. But we've got a drone now, so it's easier to catch them, and we'll be handing out fines."

He added, "And it's not just the youngsters and their bikes. Have you seen the drug dealers in their fast cars? They park in town in broad daylight to peddle their dope, and race off as soon as they see us, like it's some kind of game."

Pippa shook her head. "I can't say I've noticed ... but I've been meaning to ask you . . . you remember Alex, who died in the boar hunt?"

"Rockface? Er . . . why?"

"I read the article in *Le Télégramme* which suggested that Vicky has a lover and that they may have plotted to kill him. Is it true?"

Yann gave a long sigh. "I can assure you, Peeper, that we were not the source of that scurrilous article. Maybe your journalist friend knows who told them about the relationship between Rockface's wife and Pierre Lambert. We have interviewed both of them and have no reason to suspect that they had anything to do with the death. In fact the gendarmerie issued a statement, but the newspaper didn't publish it. Or maybe they did, but I didn't see it."

"But why is it taking so long to get the results of the ballistic tests?"

He shrugged. "These things can take time."

"Yes, but it's already been more than two weeks. Vicky is concerned. We didn't think it would take so long."

She sensed that her questions would soon run into a brick wall.

"Anyway, never mind. See you on Monday." She blew him a kiss, which he returned before shutting the door.

CHAPTER 12

Prue took her place at the head of the table, opposite Jonathan.

Emma's house was only a short walk from the centre of Carhaix. It was cramped, and the dining table had been pulled into the middle of the living room to make more space for them to sit around it.

"Shall I be mother?" Prue asked. Emma had brought in a plate of roast lamb which she'd set in the middle of the table. Jonathan gave Prue a look which indicated that his mother had stepped out of line. Prue, dressed to kill in a silk blouse tucked into tight trousers, blinked innocently.

Romy, who was small for her age and slightly overweight, sat at the opposite end of the table from Prue, scowling. She was clearly present under duress.

"Let me just serve Romy, so she can go upstairs," said Emma, aware of the tension. "I'll get the vegetables."

"Can I help?" said Prue. She pushed back her chair and almost overbalanced in her stilettos.

"No, stay where you are. I can manage. Help yourselves to wine," Emma called out from the kitchen.

Jonathan poured them both a glass of red wine and took a long sip.

"I understand you're in the same class as Luke," Prue said in English to Romy.

"*Oui.*"

"You do understand English, don't you?"

Emma, returning at that moment, answered for her daughter. "Of course she does. We've always spoken English at home, and with my parents. But she's going through a phase now and for some reason seems to prefer speaking French."

Jonathan emitted some sort of grunt. "Just like Luke, in fact."

Prue, her closely plucked eyebrows forming an arch, wanted to know why Emma had followed her parents from England and put down roots in the Breton countryside. She didn't exactly say "in the middle of nowhere" but the implication was clear. As soon as Romy had scooted upstairs, taking an ice cream cornet with her, she breezily asked Emma how long she and Jonathan had known each other. The question seemed to take him by surprise and he fixed his eyes on Emma.

"Let's see. It must be about three years, I'd say, isn't that right?" Emma said.

"Maybe more like two," he said, not wanting his mother to jump to conclusions about his culpability in the end of his marriage.

The conversation turned, as ever, to life in France as compared to England. Emma extolled the French lifestyle and the generous amount of leisure time. "I mean, in May, there are so many days off, and if a bank holiday falls on a Tuesday or a Thursday some people have four days off in a row."

"They call the long weekends *faire le pont*," Jonathan interjected. "Typical French. Having a posh expression for a long weekend."

"On the other hand, that means that I have to ask my assistant whether she wants to work," Emma went on, ignoring Jonathan's remark.

"You have a store in Carhaix, is that right?" said Prue.

"Yes. A kitchen shop. The law says that I have to shut on the first of May, but I can remain open on the other bank holidays. Sometimes I've spent the whole day alone in the store because the assistant wants the day off."

As soon as Emma got up to clear the plates away, Prue leaned towards Jonathan and said in a stage whisper, "This place is a bit of a comedown for you, isn't it?"

Before he had time to respond, she added, "Have you considered your parental responsibilities?"

"What do you mean? Of course I have." He glowered at her.

"What about you and Jennifer getting back together? I'm sure she'd take you. She's got so much on her plate, and your children need a father, particularly Mariam."

Her words had struck home. "It's none of your business, Mother. I wish you'd stop interfering in my life. I invited you here tonight so that you can meet Emma and get to know her better."

"She's very young, isn't she?" Prue went on. "Very attractive, of course."

"Not that young—"

Emma came in with a homemade lemon meringue pie and began cutting it into slices.

"Just a tiny bit for me, thanks," said Prue. She forked up a minuscule corner of her slice. "Delicious."

Emma invited her to stay for coffee, more to drink, but Prue looked at her Apple watch and exclaimed, "Goodness, look at the time!"

Jonathan offered to drive her home, but she insisted on taking a taxi. "You've had a drink or two, dear, best not."

The driver dropped her off outside the house at nine. The porch light illuminated the mauve flowers of the wisteria that festooned it. Prue went in without knocking, straight through to the kitchen. An entire Brie sat on the table.

The living room was empty, Jennifer nowhere to be seen. Wasn't it rather late to be shutting the animals in for the night? Luke must be in bed by now, and she remembered that Mariam was in Carhaix.

She heard footsteps, soft voices coming down the stairs. One was low. Definitely a man's.

She stood in the middle of the room, waiting to see who came down. Of the three of them — Prue, Jennifer, Philippe — it was hard to tell who was the most astonished.

CHAPTER 13

Jennifer stared into the fishpond, watching for movement, counting under her breath. Despite the wire netting, the heron had managed to help himself to one or more goldfish while they were all asleep.

She counted to ten. Two missing. Luke came up behind her, carrying his walking stick.

"Has he been back?" he whispered.

"Yes, I think so. Why don't we count again?"

They stared into the dark water, waiting for a glimpse of a fish emerging from under a lily pad or disturbing the weeds. After a while, they agreed that the predator had snatched two. Jennifer set about fastening the wire netting along the edge of the pond, while Luke assisted.

"How long is Granny Prue staying?"

"She's leaving tomorrow," Jennifer said. Prue had been uncharacteristically quiet since her untimely return from Jonathan and Emma's. She had never once mentioned that a man had been upstairs with Jennifer. In fact, she'd hardly spoken to Jennifer at all, focusing all her attention on the children, who were fed up with her interference. As for helping out, she'd still never found the time.

"That's why we're having the little party tonight," Jennifer said. "I thought Granny Prue might like to meet our local friends before she goes."

"Oh. Does that mean we're supposed to hand out the sandwiches?"

She smiled. "Only if you want to. But no, just be there when they come in, say 'hello' to everyone, and then you can go upstairs. Haven't you got Alain coming over?"

Luke seemed to change his best friends as frequently as his clothes.

"Yes. He's coming at five on his bike. We're going for a ride."

"Very good. And Pervenche's mum is picking up Mariam soon, which leaves us time to do some more planting. Are you going to help me with the lettuce and onions?"

He nodded enthusiastically.

"Hang on a minute. I want to check that the ewe's OK," he said, setting off to the sheep pen.

* * *

The guests, bearing bottles of wine and flowers, began trickling in a little after seven. Luke and his friend answered the door before disappearing upstairs. Noting that the gathering was smaller than the get-togethers they'd had for the panto, Meredith mentioned how much she missed her late husband, Craig. She didn't refer to her daughter, Emma, who, along with Jonathan, had not been invited.

Jennifer did the introductions for the benefit of Prue, whose face was flushed with wine and the attention.

"So you're the one whose husband was shot in the balls," she said to Vicky. Jennifer, who was handing round a plate of *rillettes* on baguettes, almost dropped the plate.

Noticing her reaction, Prue added insult to injury by saying, "Oh, did I get that wrong? I could swear that's what I was told."

Vicky turned her back on her and, helping herself to a large glass of Pinot Noir, moved away to talk to Derek and Solenn. Throughout the rest of the evening she kept glancing at Prue with an expression of startled disbelief, as if to say, "Surely this woman can't be Jonathan's mother?"

"Are there any new developments in the investigation?" Derek asked Vicky. Solenn fingered her chunky Breton necklace and stared at her.

Vicky shook her head. "As far as I know there's nothing new come up. I've started to think about the funeral but I can't decide what sort of send-off to give Alex."

Meredith, overhearing the conversation, came over to them. "Do you want a religious ceremony? Because that's what you'll get round here. Craig's funeral was a little too much so for my liking."

"I might do something back home, although his fan base is mainly here, thanks to the rock festival. I'm thinking I should give them a chance to pay their respects."

"So maybe in Carhaix then, not in the village?" said Meredith hastily, obviously alarmed at the prospect of crowds of rock fans overrunning Louennec.

"Don't worry, I'll make sure they don't pull up all the newly planted flowers," said Vicky with a laugh. "How's the campaign going? I hear there's some pushback."

Meredith pulled a face. "Yes. I got it through the council, but I've a feeling even some of those who voted for the idea haven't totally bought into it. I keep banging on about how it will be good for the village, you know, attract tourists and boost the local economy, that sort of thing. But I just hear grumbling — led by Sylvie Le Goff, I might add — about all the extra work it's causing."

Derek smiled in sympathy. "Talking of newly planted flowers, I heard from one of my French clients that there have been a couple of incidents already. They say villagers are pulling them up."

With a quick glance over her shoulder, Meredith lowered her voice. "Yes, we've had some complaints at the *mairie*.

It sounds like some of the villagers are using it as an opportunity to settle scores; the flowers are a handy weapon."

"Well, that's French village life for you," said Derek with a grin, winking at Solenn.

"Not just French, I'm sure," she responded, defensively. "As for me, I think it's a good idea, and I'm sure it will be accepted. I want the village to get three stars!"

Jennifer heard a knock at the front door and went to greet Pippa, who, as usual, was the last to arrive. She was holding a light and fluffy *tropézienne* cream cake from the bakery.

"Mother-in-law's really gone over the top tonight," Jennifer said, taking the cake. "At this point, it would give me great satisfaction to shove this into her face like a custard pie."

"Oh, you must introduce us," said Pippa, assuming an innocent smile. "Everything, er, else going all right?"

She was referring to Philippe. Jennifer grinned. "You should have seen Prue's face when she came in the other night. It was a picture."

Having deposited Pippa with Prue, who declared that she'd "heard all about" her, Jennifer took a plate of finger food to the group around Meredith. Vicky was complaining about all the things she had to sort out following Alex's death.

"What am I going to do about all his motorbikes?"

"Motorbikes?" Jennifer asked.

"Yes. He collected vintage bikes. There must be about ten in the barn. Frankly, I can't tell a Guzzi from a BMW. All I know is that Alex couldn't stand Harley-Davidsons, or their owners. He used to say they're not real bikes."

"Really? Why?" Derek asked.

"They're too heavy. He said you might as well be in a car with the window open. If you overbalance, it's curtains — you'd probably be crushed to death."

"I imagine you could make a bob or two from selling them," said Derek.

"Craig had a motorbike," Meredith said. "It was a Triumph. He didn't use it very often, only in the summer. It's still sitting in the garage getting rusty. I suppose I should sell it."

"He can't have used it much at all then," said Derek, "since summer here lasts about six weeks, if we're lucky." They all laughed.

"I'll tell you the one Alex was most proud of, though," said Vicky. "His Brough Superior. It's the same make as the one Lawrence of Arabia used to ride."

"What? The one he crashed when he died?" Derek asked. "The SS100?"

"Yes. Have you heard of it? I can show it to you if you like," Vicky said.

Derek nodded enthusiastically. "I'd love that. I've never seen one in the flesh, as it were. Those old ones are worth a fortune."

* * *

The following morning, Jennifer was up early as usual, despite a slight hangover from overdoing the Gros Plant in her efforts to ward off any more of Prue's faux pas at the party. Returning from feeding the animals, she found her mother-in-law in the kitchen, opening and shutting drawers.

"What are you looking for?"

"The cutlery. I could swear it was in this drawer."

Jennifer couldn't help replying, "I thought you'd have known where the cutlery is after all the *helping out* you've been doing."

"Temper, temper," Prue said, which had the result of making Jennifer even angrier.

"Coffee?" she asked. Without waiting for a response, she sloshed coffee into two mugs. "I hope you've packed," she said, putting sliced baguette into the toaster. Prue had dressed for the city in a tight skirt and her usual heels.

"Of course I've packed."

"I'll have to drop Luke off at school on the way to the station."

"Fine by me," said Prue. She picked up her phone and began texting. When she'd finished her coffee and toast she went upstairs, leaving Jennifer to clear away the breakfast things.

She began to wonder if she'd been too harsh on her mother-in-law, who after all was in a new place where she didn't know anyone except her family. She went upstairs to offer to take down Prue's suitcase, and found her struggling to close it.

"It's a lot heavier than when I came," said Prue. "I didn't think I'd bought that much."

"It's probably the food you put in — the saucisson. Oh, and that Breton pottery."

Prue sat on the case and finally zipped it up. "There," she said, smoothing down her skirt. She watched Jennifer wrestling the suitcase to the door on its two wheels, and went along the corridor ahead of her.

"Come on, Luke, we're going!" Jennifer called out as they passed his door.

"I'll go first," said Prue, from the top of the staircase. Behind her, Jennifer was struggling to get the hard-shell case in the right position to slide it down.

"Are you all right?" Prue asked, turning back. As she did so one of her heels gave way and she overbalanced.

Jennifer watched, aghast, as she tumbled down the stairs, landing with her head crashing against the wall. In her shock, Jennifer let go of the case which bounced down the stairs and landed on top of Prue.

Luke came out of his room and screamed, "Is Granny Prue dead?"

CHAPTER 14

Jennifer ran down the stairs. Prue lay twisted to one side beneath the heavy suitcase. She'd never have the strength to extricate her, and in any case she didn't dare.

"Shut up! Go to your room!" she said to Luke, who crept back to his bedroom.

She bent down to look at Prue, whose eyes were closed. Jennifer couldn't tell if she was breathing or not. What if a lung had collapsed from the weight of the suitcase? One leg had caught in the wooden railing and was bent back awkwardly. Seeing a bone sticking out, Jennifer panicked. She picked up Prue's arm and felt her wrist for a pulse. There didn't seem to be one. She stepped over the injured leg and ran downstairs to find her phone, which was on the kitchen table, and called the emergency services.

Then she rang Jonathan, who reacted much as she'd expected. "What have you done? OK, I'm coming right over."

* * *

Jonathan's Volvo screeched to a halt outside just after the paramedics had called for an air ambulance to take Prue to hospital.

"They think she's broken her leg and her shoulder," Jennifer told him. "But she'll be OK. She'll need emergency surgery in Brest."

"But where is the helicopter going to land?" He went over to Prue, who was lying on a stretcher, and took her hand. Her eyes were open, staring at nothing.

"She must be in shock, poor thing," he said.

"They're taking her to the playing field outside the *mairie* where the helicopter can land—"

"How did this happen?"

Jennifer resented his accusatory tone.

"We were about to set off for the station to catch the train. I was lugging her suitcase, which was incredibly heavy. She went down the stairs in front of me, overbalanced on her heels, and then fell." *I did warn her.*

"But what about the suitcase?" Jonathan asked. "How come it was lying on top of her?"

When she'd told the paramedics that her mother-in-law was English, they'd asked, "What has she got in there? The Crown Jewels?"

To Jonathan, she said, "I was so shocked that I must have let go of it, and it fell on top of her. Sorry."

Softening at the sight of her tears, Jonathan moved towards her for a hug, but she recoiled from his embrace.

"I'm not suggesting it was your fault. Of course not," he said.

Jennifer sniffed. "I've just remembered that before she fell over, she looked over her shoulder to ask me if everything was all right. She could see I was struggling. Maybe she lost her balance when she turned round."

The paramedics were loading Prue into the ambulance.

"We're off," said one.

"I'll follow you," said Jonathan, getting into his car.

He waved to Jennifer but she was already heading back into the house. Luke was staring down at them from Mariam's bedroom window.

It felt weird to be going back up the stairs. There was a dent in the plasterboard from the impact of Prue's head. One of her heels had scratched the oak varnish on a step. Jennifer shivered at the thought that she could have killed herself.

She went along the corridor and opened Luke's bedroom door. He was inside, sitting on the bed.

"Come on, little man," she said. "I'm sorry I shouted at you, but I was worried about Granny Prue. Anyway, she's going to be fine. And Daddy's gone with the paramedics to the helicopter."

"A helicopter?" At once, Luke's mood flipped from despondency to excitement. "Can we go too?"

"No, darling. I'm taking you to school. You can tell the teacher you're late because your granny had an accident."

He looked at her from under his eyebrows. "Did you push her?"

"Of course not! Why would I do a thing like that?"

"Because you don't like her."

She sat on the bed next to him and put an arm around his shoulder.

"Luke, you've been watching too much television. You don't go around killing people just because you don't like them. And how do you know that anyway?"

"I just do," he said, pouting. "Emma says so."

Bitch, thought Jennifer.

CHAPTER 15

As the day wore on, Jennifer's spirits sank further. Now she would have to add visiting her mother-in-law in hospital, an hour's drive away, to her list of things to do.

Jonathan rang just before she left to collect the children from school. She'd only just returned from taking photos of the hanging basket outside the *mairie* in Louennec for a story about Meredith's campaign. *Le Télégramme* had sent a reporter to interview the mayor about the flower competition.

"How is she?" Jennifer asked.

"I'm still at the hospital. She's out of surgery, and they say it went OK."

"Oh good. That's a relief," she said. "Have you seen her yet?"

"Not yet, no. I'll wait until I can, and then go home."

"Right. Let me know about visiting hours and stuff like that," she said, and rang off.

* * *

As soon as Mariam and Luke were back from school, Jennifer sat them down. "Look, you two, it's all hands on deck here for the foreseeable future. I want you both to pull your weight. Not only is Granny Prue in hospital, but Blackie is going to have her lambs any day now. I've got the chickens to prepare for market, *and* it's planting season."

"I'll take care of the rabbits," said Luke, getting up.

"No, I will," said Mariam. "In fact I'm going to see Lady Gaga right now."

Jennifer followed them along the path to the rabbit hutches.

"Just a second," she said. They both stopped and turned back warily. "We're going to have to be systematic about this. Let me draw up a list and we can discuss it over dinner. Who's going to set the table?"

Mariam looked at Luke.

"I'll do the animals," he said.

"Really?" said Jennifer. "OK, great. You can shut them all in for the night. Take Byron with you. He's not had any exercise all day."

"So, what about me?" Mariam asked.

"Looks like you got the short straw. Set the table, and then you can do your homework."

"But it's Friday," Mariam protested. "Pervenche is coming for a sleepover."

Jennifer had completely forgotten. They headed back towards the house, where Byron was waiting for them in the hall. Luke grabbed a stick and went outside with the dog.

Jennifer busied herself in the kitchen, chopping up tomatoes and onions to put into a meat-free pasta dish later. Behind her, Mariam was taking the knives and forks from the cutlery drawer. She was looking for the napkins when there was a knock at the front door.

"That'll be Pervenche," she said. "Let us know when dinner's ready."

Jennifer went back to preparing the vegetables. She heard the front door slam and the sound of footsteps going up the stairs. Byron came into the kitchen and slumped down on his blanket.

She stared into the back garden, where the grass still needed cutting. Was there no end to the chores?

Her thoughts turned to Philippe and his offer to lend a hand. If she hired somebody she'd be liable for the hefty social contributions that having an employee entailed, and she didn't like to risk paying a helper *au noir*. But if it was a friend doing the work, she wouldn't have to declare it, would she? Maybe Philippe could prepare the chickens for market? That would be a start at least, and it was only once a month. But she didn't like to impose on him. On the other hand, he had offered, hadn't he?

She searched the playlists on her phone and found some calming jazz. But the peace was short-lived. Soon, the children clattered downstairs for dinner. Mariam and Pervenche had adopted the annoying habit of talking in *verlan*, a slang in which the syllables of words were reversed, so that adults couldn't understand what they were saying. Jennifer had noticed that the two of them called each other *meuf*, meaning *femme*.

Mariam sat down at the table and, with a wink to Pervenche, turned to Jennifer to ask, "What's for dinner, *meuf*?"

It was the last straw. Jennifer slammed down the pasta dish on the table. "Enough! First of all, I'm not your *meuf*, I'm your mother. You two can stop being so rude."

With a sideways glance at each other, the two girls hung their heads in silence. Luke then took it into his head to refuse vegetables, and would only eat his dinner when she promised him ice cream afterwards. By the time dinner was over, the dishwasher loaded and the children back upstairs, her nerves were shredded.

She returned to the kitchen table to draw up a timetable of tasks the children could do without impinging on their leisure activities. After all, it wouldn't hurt if they knew where the money was coming from. It was something she and Jonathan should have done years ago. Even as the smallholding expanded, they'd continued to sort out their duties on a daily basis. What a pair of amateurs they'd been.

She'd just underlined the heading *Sheep* in her notebook when her phone rang. It was Pippa.

"You busy?" she asked.

"I've had to make dinner for children who are now trolling me in *verlan*. I'm drawing up a work programme for the kids and trying to find some help on the farm," she said. "And I've got to ask the gendarmerie if I can take a picture of the new drone they're using, for the paper. Oh, and my mother-in-law's fallen down the stairs and broken half her bones. Apart from that, I've nothing to do."

"Your mother-in-law?" Jennifer got the feeling from Pippa's tone of voice that she also suspected she'd been pushed.

"Don't worry, she'll survive," Jennifer said. "What's up?"

Pippa was speaking in a low voice. "Hold on, I'm just stepping outside the bakery for some privacy." There were a few moments' silence. "You'll never believe what Yann just told me when he came in for his baguette!"

"What?"

"They got the forensics back on the ballistics, and it turns out that the bullet that killed Alex doesn't match any of the guns the hunters were using."

Jennifer wrote down *not the hunters* and underlined it.

"So that means—"

"Yes!" Pippa was almost squeaking in her excitement. "It was somebody else."

CHAPTER 16

As Meredith approached the meeting room, leaning on a cane, she could hear the murmur of voices from inside. She was even more nervous than usual, because the first point on the agenda was the *commune*'s application for the France in Bloom competition.

More complaints had reached her desk, and she'd had to insist that Sylvie Le Goff followed these up. She wanted to know whether it was an organised opposition, or individual villagers egging each other on. She'd noticed that a couple of the front gardens belonging to houses on Louennec's small high street had been ransacked, and worried that matters were escalating.

She opened the door and took her seat, placing her bad leg sideways. The councillors looked at her expectantly as she called the meeting to order.

"You'll be pleased to hear that our application for the Villes et Villages Fleuris has been accepted by the authorities in Quimper. Thank you, Jean-Michel, for putting it together. Now we've got to get started! I've invited a landscape architect from the *département* to come over to discuss our ideas."

Out of the corner of her eye, she spotted Sylvie exchanging a glance with a farmer, who raised his eyes to heaven.

"It has come to our notice that not everyone in the village shares our enthusiasm for this project," Meredith went on. "So, it is up to all of us to engage with the villagers and promote it. Once again, we should remember that this isn't just about flowers."

She explained some of the initiatives in the council's application. "For a start, we're planning a cycle path along the river, with some benches alongside. It won't cost much and will provide a convivial space for villagers of all ages. We're going to talk to the primary school about the children devising a couple of notices about the wildlife.

"The signs will point out such things as, er," she had no idea of the French words for kingfisher and dragonfly, "birds, and the insects to be found along the river. Are we agreed that this is a good idea? That would cover the educational aspect in the application criteria."

Most of the councillors nodded. They seemed to like the idea. "And for environmental reasons we'll be installing rainwater tanks around the village. It's all about sustainability.

"Promoting biodiversity is another of the competition's criteria, so we're going to approach people with large gardens and ask them to plant wildflowers to encourage bees and other insects. We're considering hedgehog tunnels too, so that they can cross the road in safety."

She heard an indignant "*pff!*" from the far end of the table. She couldn't see the culprit but presumed it must be Armel, the dairy farmer, expressing his opinion of *le wokisme*. Not for the first time, she was aware of the battle lines around the table between the "townies" and the country folk.

"We shall also be planting five saplings along the main street. It will be a type of cherry that doesn't drop sap on to cars — and they'll look very pretty in the spring."

"What about les Charpentiers?" one councillor asked.

"The *charpentiers*?" What about them? Meredith couldn't see what relevance the neighbourhood carpenters had, before realising it was somebody's name. She glanced at Sylvie, who hadn't mentioned these people to her. Was it an ambush?

"They saw the intruders in their garden," he said. "I've got the video capture from their webcam. They're not happy about having to buy one in the first place, but they'd already had their peonies pulled up two weeks ago."

"I'm so sorry to hear that, Claude," said Meredith. "May I see this video?"

Claude handed his phone to Meredith with fingers darkened by nicotine. The grainy image, lasting about thirty seconds, showed two shadowy figures systematically uprooting busy Lizzies from a flowerbed and tossing them on to the street.

"Where do they live?" Meredith asked. "Have they put in a complaint?"

She turned to Sylvie, who shook her head.

"It's a young couple on our street, Le Chemin du Lys," said Claude. It was a quiet street on the far side of Louennec. "People are going to start taking the law into their own hands if these attacks aren't stopped."

Again, Meredith glanced at Sylvie. She didn't want to commit a procedural error.

"Look, I can approach the authorities in Carhaix. It seems we need to ask for additional police patrols here. I believe that's been done before, isn't that right, Sylvie?"

Mme Le Goff nodded.

"Right. So can you do this through the proper channels?"

Mme Le Goff sighed and wrote something in her notebook.

"Thank you," Meredith said pointedly. She returned the phone to Claude. "Maybe the others would like to see this. Why don't you ask Claude after this meeting? The question is, did your neighbours recognise the intruders?"

He shrugged. "How could they? They were wearing balaclavas."

Meredith sat back in her chair and made a note. "The other question is, should we publicise this, er, desecration? Or do you think we'd run the risk of copycat attacks if we did?"

Everyone spoke at once.

"Jean-Michel?" she asked, turning to her deputy who was sitting beside her.

"I think let the police deal with it," he said. "Then we'll see. But I must say that given the number of complaints we've received, there could be a gang of vigilantes at work here."

"They're not stealing the plants though, are they?" Meredith asked.

"No. It's simply gratuitous violence, definitely linked to our application," said Jean-Michel. He raised his hands in the air, as if to say, *C'est la France*.

* * *

The meeting came to an end with a general scraping of chairs on the parquet floor. Meredith, pursing her lips in pain as she stood up, left the hall carrying the briefcase she'd inherited from Craig. Mme Le Goff was waiting for her just outside.

"This situation could easily get out of control," said Sylvie in a low voice, her thin lips in a tight line. "You'll have noticed that your campaign is not popular here."

Meredith couldn't prevent her anger boiling over. "What do you mean, *my* campaign? If you recall, this initiative was passed through a vote of the entire council. That's democracy, Sylvie. And I believe that the majority of villagers do support Louennec in Bloom. It's up to us to persuade the doubters, that's all."

Without a word, Mme Le Goff strode away. Jean-Michel caught up with Meredith just as she reached her car, swaying on her stick.

"Are you OK?" he asked.

"Nothing serious," she said. "I get these gout spells from time to time."

Jean-Michel winced in sympathy.

"What did she want?" he said. She knew he was probably the only councillor she could trust, and she relied on his advice. He'd earned her gratitude for switching sides to join her election campaign, thereby ensuring the defeat of the outgoing mayor who had been a staunch defender of the controversial wind farm project. Meredith's election had taken the sting out of the issue, which was now working its way slowly through the regional bureaucracy.

"Oh, she was just pointing out, in her inimitable way, that the France in Bloom campaign isn't going down too well in the village. For goodness' sake, we're only talking about making a couple of improvements!"

"They don't like change here," he said. "I think the key is to persuade the younger ones who work in town; it's the older villagers and the farmers who are so set in their ways."

"I hope you're right, Jean-Michel," she said, opening her car door. "Maybe we should find a way of setting about it systematically. I'm fed up with Sylvie constantly saying 'this isn't how we do things here'."

"By the way, I heard today that there's been a development in the investigation into the shooting of your friend, Alex."

She threw her briefcase on to the back seat and waited to hear the news.

"The police have been unable to trace the gun that fired the fatal shot," he said.

"Oh. That's bad news. Vicky will be disappointed."

"I know. At least it means that we're all in the clear. The hunters, I mean. Those of us who were there that day."

"Do you think they'll be able to find the killer?"

Jean-Michel shrugged. "I wouldn't bet on it. Most of the villagers in Louennec have a hunting rifle. What are the gendarmes going to do? Test each one? They've probably got more urgent problems on their hands."

CHAPTER 17

Vicky heard the front door slam, followed by footsteps on the stone floor. Which one of her staff could it be this time, come to jump out of the shadows at her? She really needed to have a word with them about the way they crept around the property.

She put down the knife with which she was preparing vegetables for that evening. The kitchen door opened, and Pierre entered. Normally he let her know before he came over, so she was surprised to see him.

"What's happened?" she asked him. "Do you want a cup of tea? Something stronger?"

She went over to kiss him on the cheeks. They were damp with sweat.

"Come and sit down."

He pulled up a stool at the counter and wiped his forehead with the back of his hand.

"Been working hard in the field, have you?" she asked.

"Ha. If only," he said in English. He said something in French that made her check the translation on her phone. Hemp field, was it?

"They've got me," he announced dramatically — in English this time.

"Who has?" Vicky was rapidly growing exasperated.

"*Les flics*. The game's up. The gendarmes sent up their drone over my field. They have found the cannabis."

"What are you talking about, Pierre? What cannabis?"

He fastened a calculating gaze upon her. Then he cleared his throat and explained that he'd been growing cannabis in the middle of the hemp crop in his field.

"Oh. I see." Except that she didn't. What was the big deal? Dope had been part of her life for as long as she could remember.

"This is very serious, Vicky. In France it's strictly forbidden to grow it. Do you understand me? It's a crime."

"Even for your personal use? How ridiculous!"

He shot her a fierce look. "It wasn't for me. I got more money for that cannabis than I did for my hemp. I risk a big fine, and possibly even jail."

"Jail? Oh no!" She gave him a hug. "I'm sure it won't come to that."

"I hope I can persuade them of that. It's the first time I've been caught. *Putain!*"

* * *

After Pierre had gone home, Vicky went to the bakery in search of a cake.

"Have you made any *tropéziennes* today?" she asked Pippa. "I'm having a couple of friends over tonight, and it would save me the trouble of baking."

"You're in luck," said Pippa. She went into the back and returned, the cake balanced on one hand, and began putting it into a cardboard container. "These days, I mainly bake them to order. Some ribbon, maybe?" she added, with a wink.

Vicky also asked for two baguettes, and took out her card to pay.

"How are the funeral arrangements going?" Pippa asked, watching her tap.

"Didn't I tell you? Oh yeah, it's going to be big. I've arranged for a horse and cart to take Alex to the crem in Carhaix. It'll be covered with flowers, you know like in the East End. That's where he was from, you see."

She raised a hand. "No need for a receipt, thanks darlin'. He used to drive me mad, actually, with his Cockney slang. Like, he'd be talking about maybe selling one of his bikes, saying a Billy would come along. I thought he meant someone called Billy, until he told me it meant a punter. Billy Bunter? Geddit?"

Pippa rolled her eyes heavenward.

"Exactly. A real pain, I tell you," said Vicky.

"But what about the fans? They're not all going to fit into the hall at the crem, are they?"

"That's what I thought. I put a notice in the local rag and they sent someone over to interview me, what with Alex being well known and all. Jennifer took the picture. I think she said the article is going in tomorrow. So, the fans can pay their respects in the street on the way to the service, while a smallish group of us go inside for the ceremony. Nothing religious, mind."

"Oh, right. I see," said Pippa. "We'd better get there early for a seat then. The hall could still be overflowing."

"I want you and Jennifer to join me behind the coffin — for company, if that's all right. I've invited Meredith too, for moral support. And Alex's children will be coming over."

"Of course," Pippa said.

About to go, Vicky stopped at the door.

"Oh, and about Pierre," she said. "I presume you heard he's in the clear over Alex's murder, along with all the other hunters, of course. After he was smeared in the paper like that, I was worried, to tell you the truth."

"Yes, I did hear. So, they're back to square one then," Pippa said.

Vicky stepped back inside. "Well, he might be in the clear regarding Alex, but he's got another problem."

"Nothing serious, I hope," said Pippa.

"I'm afraid it is. You know that drone the gendarmes have got?"

Pippa nodded. "You mean the one they use when those yobs are causing havoc with their motorbikes?"

"Not only that, I've just found out they use it for all sorts of surveillance. Jennifer spent an afternoon with them recently, taking photos."

"But what's this got to do with Pierre?" Pippa was suddenly conscious that she was wasting time gossiping while Gwen needed help with the next batch of bread.

Vicky hesitated. "I hope this is kept out of the paper, given what happened the last time. You see, he's being done for growing cannabis."

"Cannabis? What? Where?" Pippa glanced over her shoulder. "Just give me a sec, I must check that Gwen's OK. We're going to be busy soon."

She disappeared into the back.

"So what's going on?" she asked, returning after a couple of minutes, and leaning over the counter.

"Well, he's got a hemp field. I didn't know — obviously — but apparently, the hemp crop only grows round the edge of the field. The rest is given over to cannabis. The drone spotted the plastic covering."

What an idiot. "Oh, I'm so sorry," Pippa said.

"So that's it. And now he's being investigated and he could be sent to jail! I told him I'd help out with any fine. But jail for a piddling thing like that — I don't Adam and Eve it, as Alex would say!"

Pippa scrutinised Vicky's face, which bore the signs of a life lived at top speed, for more clues. In her opinion there was no smoke without fire, and this was the second time Pierre had been under suspicion, rightly or wrongly.

"He's a bit younger than you, isn't he?" She realised how indiscreet the question sounded, but Vicky was unoffended. "Yes, ten years younger. So what?"

"So what indeed," said Pippa. Vicky and Alex had lived in another world. Who knew what went on there?

She watched Vicky cross the street and get into the car with her pastries. What if Pierre was a wrong'un? What if he and Vicky had actually conspired to cause Alex's death?

She remembered how shaken Pierre had seemed on the night of the boar hunt. Was he simply shocked at seeing his friend fatally wounded, or had he returned to the mansion to report back to Vicky?

She was struck by an even more sobering thought. Could it be that Vicky's grief at Alex's death was all a charade?

CHAPTER 18

Jennifer found Prue dozing in her hospital bed. She had her left leg raised by a pulley contraption and her right shoulder was swathed in bandages.

She opened her eyes.

"Oh, you made it, then," she said in a tone that may or may not have been sarcastic.

"How are you feeling?" Jennifer asked.

"I've got so many pins, screws and metal plates in me that I'll rattle if ever they let me out of here," she replied, grimacing. "I can't believe I've been here a week already."

"Are you still in pain?"

Prue's eyes narrowed. "Of course I'm in pain. Why d'you think I'm in hospital?"

"The nurse says it's only a couple more days. They're finding you a place for rehab, so it won't be long now."

Jennifer had been mightily relieved to learn that her mother-in-law wasn't going to be landing on her doorstep to recover.

"I've got the insurance to thank for that," said Prue. "At least I'm not at the mercy of the NHS."

"Yes, let's count our blessings." Jennifer looked around the room. Prue was still on a drip. In one corner a machine

beeped gently. A jug of water and the remains of some inde-
terminate puree on a plastic plate were on the overbed table.

"Jonathan brought those," said Prue, noticing Jennifer's
glance fall on a vase of peonies.

"Can I get you anything?" she asked. "A drink of water?
Something from the shop?"

"Give me some of that water," Prue commanded. Jennifer
poured out the drink and put the plastic cup to her lips. The
liquid went down the wrong way and Prue coughed, spitting
it into Jennifer's face.

She backed away. "Let's try again," she said, wondering if
Prue was really capable of doing something like that on purpose.

At that point a nurse came in and took command. Prue
smiled as though butter wouldn't melt in her mouth.

"*Merci*," she said, watching the nurse take away her tray.

Jennifer got up to go. It would take her an hour to drive
home.

"Thank you for coming." Prue sank back on to the pil-
low with a sigh. "And give my love to the children."

* * *

Philippe was already at work in the potato patch when
Jennifer got home. Byron was stretched out nearby, keeping
an eye on things. He raised his head and wagged his tail
slowly as she approached.

"I've done the chickens," said Philippe. He stopped digging and leaned on his fork. "It wasn't a big job."

She went over and kissed him. When she'd given him
the grand tour of the property, she'd shown him her "lab"
where she prepared the chickens for market, but she hadn't
meant it as a hint.

"Really? You took them out of the run? Clever you. That's
really kind. I took care of the other six already, so they're ready
for market."

"This is none of my business," he added, "but you
should put a better lock on the chicken runs."

"Yes, I know," she said, embarrassed. They currently had elasticated straps that hooked round the gates to hold them shut. "I guess I never got round to replacing them."

"I can find something for you," he offered. "These days you never know who'll come looking for stuff to steal, including farm equipment. I have a farmer friend who's just spent five thousand euros on security. He's put cameras everywhere."

"What?!" Jennifer exclaimed.

"People think it's safe in the countryside, but look at those Romanian gangs who come over and clear out the mushrooms in the forests every autumn. They shake down the apples from people's orchards."

She grimaced. "You're right. But you can't put locks on orchards, can you?"

He grinned.

"But really, you shouldn't be doing this." She pointed at a crate of potatoes that was almost full.

"They're ready, though. No point in waiting."

Jennifer hesitated. She felt like she was abusing Philippe's generosity.

"Let me help you — though I've got to go and collect the children in about half an hour."

She went to the toolshed and pulled out another fork. They worked in silence, lifting the potatoes from the crumbly soil into the crate. It was hot work. Philippe's discarded jacket lay on the ground where he'd dropped it.

"What about us?" said Philippe eventually. "When will you have time to see me?"

"Well, I had a lucky escape today. I was worried that they'd send my mother-in-law back here after she was discharged from hospital. That would have been a disaster."

They both laughed.

"What about your place?" she asked. "Maybe after the market? My kids will be with their father."

"I'll need to tidy up first," he said.

"Maybe you could show me your cellars? I'd be really interested to see them."

"What's your favourite cheese?" he asked.

"Mmm, let's see. I think it's Mont d'Or. It's delicious and so runny that you scoop it out with a spoon."

"Good choice," he said. "I was going to offer you some. But it's getting towards the end of the season. I thought you were going to say Brie."

She smiled. "Of course. Brie is supposed to be the queen of cheeses, isn't it? So creamy when it's ripe."

She still wasn't sure whether Philippe was a cheesemaker or an *affineur* who specialised in ripening and storing cheese. She suspected he was probably the latter.

"So, tell me, how did you get into the cheese business?" she asked.

He stopped digging and stood with his foot on the fork, wiping his forehead with his sleeve.

"My dad had a cattle farm. When I was a kid, I always got attached to the calves, and my heart broke every time they were taken away to the slaughterhouse."

"Ah, I see," said Jennifer. She could imagine how upset the young Philippe must have been, knowing how attached the children became to their rabbits.

"There was one heifer in particular," Philippe went on. "I called her Thrush; she used to lick my hand. It was a strange feeling, her thick tongue rasped on my skin, but I liked it. I thought I'd die when the lorry came for her." He paused for a moment, gazing into the distance. "After that, I decided not to follow in my father's footsteps. I went to work on a dairy farm, which got me interested in cheese. Then I went to work with a cheesemonger in town, who showed me the ropes, and became an *affineur*."

"Do you know which is my favourite?" he asked.

Jennifer thought for a moment, and shrugged. "*Je donne ma langue au chat*," one of her favourite French expressions: "I give my tongue to the cat", or in other words, "I give up."

"Saint-Nectaire," he said. "It has a crust, but inside it has plenty of personality and a slightly nutty taste."

"You sound like a connoisseur of fine wines," she said. "Look at the time! I'd better go."

She pretended to hold up a camera: "Say cheese." Philippe gave her a slightly puzzled smile.

"That's how we Brits get somebody to smile for a photo," she explained. "I don't suppose it works with *fromage*."

"Oh, I see," Philippe said. "For us it's *ouistiti*."

"*Ouistiti?* What on earth does that mean?" Jennifer asked.

"It's a kind of monkey." He pushed his fork into the soil and resumed digging.

"You can stop now," she said. "You've done more than enough today."

"You go. I'll finish this job," he said, and winked. "See you on Saturday, at the market."

Jennifer walked back to the car, jingling the keys in her pocket. It took only minutes to drive to the village, where she found Luke talking to a couple of friends outside the school gate.

They drove on to Carhaix to pick up Mariam. She came out, talking animatedly to a busty girl, presumably from her class. Maybe she'd made a new friend. Progress at last.

"Who was that?" she asked Mariam as she got into the car.

"Ivy," Mariam said.

"Ivy? So she's English." Mariam nodded. "What happened to Pervenche?"

"Oh, she's *en couple*." In a couple? At thirteen? Staring at her daughter, Jennifer almost swerved. Mariam added airily, "Keep your hair on. She's got a boyfriend, that's all."

Jennifer glanced anxiously at Mariam, who was fiddling with her hair, apparently unconcerned at this turn of events. Luke, meanwhile, kept up his usual flow of chatter from the back seat, dipping into a bag of Haribos. As they drove past the side of the smallholding, Jennifer saw Philippe, still digging out potatoes.

"Who's that man, Mummy?" Luke asked. "And what's Byron doing there with him?"

"It's Philippe, one of Mummy's friends from the market. The cheesemonger, you know?" she said. "He's helping out a bit on the smallholding."

She glanced at her children in the rear-view mirror and intercepted a look of dismay. The evening ahead was going to be tricky. She parked the car and the children got out — Mariam heading straight for the house while Luke made his way to the potato patch, no doubt to interrogate Philippe. But something caught his eye as he passed the sheep meadow.

He ran back to the car, shouting, "Mummy! It's Blackie. She's having the babies!"

CHAPTER 19

Jennifer raced to the sheep pen, where the ewe, named for the colour of her head, was lying on her side. Luke was practically jumping up and down with excitement.

"Are you going to call the vet?" he asked.

"It may not be necessary." It was Philippe, coming up behind them. He got down on to his knees and stroked the animal's belly. "Look, she's in the final stages. This one is almost out."

"Luke, go inside. We'll take care of this," said Jennifer. "And take Byron with you."

Luke whistled to the dog, who followed him back to the house. No sooner had he disappeared than Blackie's waters burst. Jennifer felt slightly queasy. Her only previous experience of a sheep giving birth had been when she and Jonathan had lost a lamb and had had to call the vet.

Philippe looked up. "She'll be OK. Here he comes. Can you see the two front legs and his little head?"

She got on to her knees beside him. "Tell me what to do."

"With a bit of luck, she won't need our help."

Jennifer went off to collect the lambing kit, which consisted of a bucket of water, a cloth, some disinfectant and a broom, along with a rubbish bag for the afterbirth.

She and Philippe watched the heaving animal deliver two small lambs in a pool of yuck. To her surprise, Jennifer was overcome with joy. She cleared up the mess and said, "I'm going to get Luke. He'll want to see this, he's been driving us mad for the past month."

As she left the pen, she said over her shoulder, "I don't know what I'd have done without you. You've saved me a fortune in vet's fees."

"*Oui, ça coûte la peau des fesses*," said Philippe with a smile. So, the skin from one's buttocks is worth a lot of money, is it? She grinned. Another delightful expression to memorise. Her idiomatic French was progressing in leaps and bounds thanks to her new relationship.

Luke didn't need telling twice. He raced to the field ahead of her.

"Come on, Mummy, look!" he called out. They gazed in wonderment as the two baby lambs struggled to their feet. Philippe gently guided the lambs to the sheep's teats and they began to feed.

"Wow," said Luke. "What are we going to call them?"

Whatever you like, Jennifer thought. She wanted to give Philippe a hug, but didn't dare in front of Luke.

"You decide," she said to her son.

Jennifer's phone rang. It was Pippa.

"Sorry to bother you but . . ."

Jennifer moved further into the sheep meadow, away from the others, keeping a safe distance from Rambo. They all steered clear of the old ram after he had fatally injured a younger rival the previous year.

"No problem. We're just celebrating the arrival of two little lambs."

"Oh, congratulations. I just wanted to meet you to talk about Alex's death — and about Pierre in particular."

"Of course." She was on the point of suggesting they meet at the café after the market when she remembered that she was supposed to be seeing Philippe.

"Just let me know when you're free," she said. "And I'll see you at the funeral tomorrow."

She rang off, thinking about how, in the countryside, life and death are so intertwined. Today they were celebrating a birth, and the very next day, they'd be mourning a loss.

Back in the pen, Philippe was tidying up, throwing a layer of straw on the ground and giving the mother some fresh hay, while Luke peppered him with questions.

"Don't let him bother you," she said to Philippe. She hesitated. "Would you like to stay to dinner?" *No, not yet, it's too soon.*

"Thank you, but I'd better get back," he said.

CHAPTER 20

Carhaix had never seen anything like it. Alex's coffin, crowned by a wreath of white lilies, processed slowly through the town in an open carriage drawn by a carthorse. A man in a black morning suit and a top hat drove the carriage through the watching crowds, looking straight ahead.

Vicky, draped from head to toe in what looked like a black net curtain, followed on foot at the head of the funeral procession. Behind her came her village friends and Alex's two children from his first marriage, both now in their twenties. The two of them were as unlike "Rockface" as it was possible to be. They were smartly dressed, the son in a suit, and the daughter in a grey jacket and trousers. Meredith wore her tricolour sash in her official capacity as representative of the *commune*.

The narrow pavements were crammed with metalheads and goths, all in black skinny jeans and T-shirts bearing different satanic logos. Vicky turned to acknowledge their shouts of "Rockface" as the procession advanced. Their white faces contrasted with the weatherbeaten features of the locals who had ventured into the crowd. They flung flowers onto the coffin as it passed. Soon it was topped by a mountain of carnations and lilies.

Pippa saw Yann and another gendarme watching the proceedings from a spot with a good view of the procession. He gave her a wink and a smile as she passed.

Suddenly, something flew through the air and landed on the coffin with a bang.

"What on earth was that?" Jennifer asked Pippa. They craned their necks to see. It was a supermarket chicken, still wrapped in plastic. Why would anyone throw a chicken on to a coffin? But the goths applauded the tribute, with still more cries of "Rockface!"

As the cortège drew nearer to the crematorium, the shouting got louder.

"What's going on? What are they saying?" Pippa asked.

The tributes to Alex had been replaced by something more vulgar.

"They're swearing at each other," Jennifer replied. At that point, a clump of yellow rapeseed hit Meredith on the head, knocking her off balance. Brushing soil from her hair, she searched the crowd for the culprit, but whoever it was had disappeared. She walked on, struggling to maintain her dignity, until a man yelled, almost in her ear, "*On ne veut pas de ton projet!*" This prompted a youth on the opposite side of the street to swear at the protester, apparently referring to his mother's private parts.

"*Va te faire foutre!*" responded the other, shaking his fist at him.

Alarmed, Vicky glanced over her shoulder at Jennifer and Pippa. By now, instead of tossing their flower tributes on to the coffin, the citizens were throwing them at each other. A bouquet of roses wrapped in brown paper caught the horse's flank. It reared up on its hind legs and bolted. The driver stood up on his seat and pulled with all his might on the reins, but the terrified animal careered down the slope, towards the crematorium.

Vicky flung off her netting, revealing bare tattooed arms, torn black jeans and a hellfire T-shirt. Followed by the rest of the procession, she ran towards the hall past two officials who were standing at the entrance, aghast.

Meanwhile, the carthorse was galloping round the grave-yard as if it were a racetrack, the coffin swinging precariously from side to side. By the time the driver finally got it under control, the flowers lay scattered on the graves that it had bolted across. The horse came to a standstill near the chapel, snorting and tossing its head.

The driver got down and calmed the horse, while the pallbearers rushed out to attend to the coffin. The protesters having evaporated, the mourners attempted to recover their dignity.

"*Mes excuses, madame,*" the funeral director said to Vicky, whose eyes were pinned on the coffin, one hand raised to her heart. "*Voulez-vous bien me suivre?*"

She followed him inside, her netting trailing behind her like a train.

* * *

Forty-five minutes later they re-emerged, the mourners form-ing a line to pay their respects to Vicky and Alex's family before departing.

Once the line had dispersed, Vicky came over to Pippa and Jennifer, who were standing with the other members of their little community.

"How are you, Vicky? It was a lovely ceremony, and so moving to hear Alex's music," said Pippa, presuming that the deafening sounds that they'd just listened to inside were the departed's greatest hits. "But why did they throw a chicken on to the coffin? I've never seen anything like it."

"Oh that," said Vicky. "Back in the old days, Alex once bit the head off a chicken while he was performing at a con-cert. I assumed that's what it was about. It's the sort of thing the fans remember. You know, like when Ozzy Osbourne bit the head off a bat?"

"He didn't, did he?" said Pippa, shaking her head.

"Alex must have been smiling in his coffin when it landed. But what the fuck happened on the way down to the crem?" said Vicky. "A chicken is one thing, but Alex would never have expected a near riot at his funeral."

They turned to see Meredith approach.

"Did you recognise the bastard who threw that plant at you?" Vicky asked her.

"I'm afraid I didn't," said Meredith, adjusting her sash. "Evidently, not everyone is happy with our plans to beautify Louennec. I'm sure they came along on purpose, just to cause trouble, knowing I'd be there. But we're not changing course."

Vicky caught sight of Derek, who was about to leave with Solenn, and called out to him. "Derek, if you want to join us, why don't we all go back to the house and chill with a drink and something to eat? I didn't want to do anything more formal, I thought the procession would be enough."

"With pleasure," he said, with a glance at Solenn, who nodded.

They waited while Vicky sorted out the collection of Alex's ashes. When she came out, ten of them squeezed into two people carriers provided by the funeral home and headed to the mansion, while the stragglers took a cab. Pierre sat in Vicky's car next to her and Pippa, who reflected that the grieving widow was no longer concealing their relationship. She wondered whether Alex's son and daughter, squeezed into the back of the van, had any idea of what was going on.

Vicky's staff had laid on a lavish spread. The dining-room table heaved with dishes of beautifully arranged shellfish, cold cuts and cheeses.

"Help yourselves," Vicky said, while a young woman in a maid's uniform began handing out drinks on a tray. "Red, white or soft drink," she added. "I didn't think champagne seemed appropriate today."

"Well, it was a great send-off," said Jennifer, raising a glass. "A bit unconventional . . ."

The guests all laughed, as if funerals with goths and metalheads and loud rock music were an everyday occurrence in their village. The drink flowed and the conversation grew animated.

Pippa stood next to Jennifer, near the oysters. She put a squeeze of lemon onto one and slurped it down. "Delicious."

"So, do you still want to talk to me about him?" Jennifer asked, with a glance in the direction of Pierre, who was standing with Vicky and chatting with Meredith's deputy, Jean-Michel.

"I did, yes. I just can't help thinking that he might be the murderer," said Pippa.

"You mean, *he* killed Alex?"

Jennifer followed Pippa's lead and swallowed an oyster, before moving away from the table to let Solenn help herself.

"Yes. Because although the ballistics tests showed that the murder weapon didn't belong to any of the hunters, what if they've got more than one gun?"

"Just a sec, Pippa. Don't you think the police would have searched their homes? We've been through this before. I can't see how it could have been any of the people who were there that day. They were all Alex's friends, for a start."

"Would they bother to search the hunters' homes, now they've got the results? Vicky thinks they've made up their minds that it was a hunting accident, so they can't be bothered to carry out a thorough investigation."

"Hmm." Jennifer cast her eyes over the table. "My God, she's got lobster rolls there."

They each grabbed a roll.

"He might look like a nice guy," Pippa continued, "but he's into stuff which isn't exactly legal."

"Like what?"

"Apparently, he's being done for growing cannabis. Vicky told me," Pippa said.

"What, really? Where?"

"He's got this hemp field. Do you remember, it belonged to Didier, who led the wind farm protests?" Pippa said.

"Growing hemp is perfectly legal, you know," Jennifer said.

"I know that. But the police drone spotted cannabis growing in the middle of it."

Jennifer laughed. "Look, I think it's rather a stretch to say that because he's growing a bit of cannabis, he's the sort of person who'd commit a murder."

"I'm just saying that maybe he shouldn't be ruled out, that's all," Pippa said.

"And what does Yann say?" Jennifer asked.

Pippa pouted. "I haven't actually asked him. You know how he reacts, as though I'm telling him how to do his job? I know how I'd feel if he did the same to me."

Jennifer grinned.

Vicky clapped her hands, and the chatter died down.

"Excuse me, everybody. Derek has just reminded me that I'd promised to show him Alex's vintage motorbike collection. If anyone else wants a look, now's your chance."

They all filed out of the house and down a gravel drive which led to a large converted barn with double doors. Vicky took out a set of keys from her jeans pocket and pushed back the doors. The interior of the barn was filled mainly with motorcycles, tools and farm machinery stored at the back.

"There you are. Here are his beauties," she said.

Derek went in first, moving from one bike to another. They were all draped in dust covers. He lifted each one, stroking the saddle of a Triumph T120R as he wandered from bike to bike. Meredith followed him round out of curiosity, remembering Craig's love of motorcycles.

Vicky chatted at the door with Pippa and Jennifer. Alex's son, standing with his sister, kept checking his watch as though they had a train to catch. The French contingent, consisting of Pierre, Jean-Michel and Solenn, stood on the other side of the entrance arguing with each other about something with exaggerated hand gestures.

"How come you're so knowledgeable?" Meredith murmured to Derek.

"I used to have a bike when I was young," he said. "But I sold it after I had an accident. It wasn't a vintage motorcycle like these." He lifted another cover and admired an old BMW.

"Look at this one," he said to Meredith. She gazed at the black bike, then back to Derek.

"How much would this be worth then?" she asked.

"This is an R69S, see?" She nodded.

"It was a classic touring bike from the 1960s. I reckon one like this in good nick would sell for almost fifty thousand euros now," he said.

"You're kidding me," said Meredith. Derek shook his head. He turned round and called out to Vicky, "But where's the Brough?"

"The what?" said Vicky.

"The Brough Superior SS100. The one you mentioned, the same model as the T. E. Lawrence bike. It would be worth a lot more than these others, it could fetch as much as half a million."

"What? Are you serious?" Vicky took a step back, staring at him in surprise. "Why so much?"

"Because of their rarity. Did you know that T. E. Lawrence called each of his Brough's 'George', after the guy who made them?"

"How come Alex never mentioned any of this to me?"

Derek smiled. "He probably thought you weren't interested."

But Vicky was no longer listening; she'd gone to the back of the barn, where the mini digger was parked, in search of the bike. Derek followed her, raising the dust cover of each motorcycle as he went.

"Well, it's not here," he said, eventually.

"What do you mean it's not here?" she said. She stopped looking and turned to face him. Then she saw it.

Oil on the ground, where a motorcycle once stood. The Brough had gone.

CHAPTER 21

The newspapers had a field day with the pandemonium at Alex's funeral. The front page of *Le Télégramme* was dominated by pictures of the streets of Carhaix strewn with flowers left by the pitched battles of the previous day.

Rockface funeral overshadowed by war of the flowers, the headline read. The story went on to relate how the mayor of Louennec had drawn the ire of some in the *commune* with her plans to take part in the France in Bloom contest. Meredith was quoted as saying that she would stand firm in the face of the opposition and that the majority of villagers supported the project. She didn't mention the humiliating attack by a plant.

Pippa and Yann had dinner that night at the pizzeria behind the Carhaix town hall. Yann sipped a *bol* of Breton cider, Pippa a glass of red wine.

"So, what do you think?" Pippa began, watching the cheese from the pizza drip through Yann's fingers. He smiled. He knew what was coming.

"About what?" He wiped his fingers with a paper napkin and reached out to take her hand.

"You know perfectly well. What on earth was all that about yesterday?"

"The flower riot? It wasn't spontaneous, was it? At least it didn't look that way," he said.

"Do you know who any of the troublemakers were?"

"Oh yes."

"Even the person who threw the rapeseed at Meredith? I can't believe it's come to this, I mean, a stupid flower competition. Really!"

Yann frowned. "It was a guy called Tanguy Seznec, a handyman who lives in Kerivac."

Pippa had been to Kerivac, a hamlet not far from Louennec known for its standing stones.

"Peeper, it's about more than a stupid flower competition, as you call it. In fact, according to what we saw, the projectile was aimed at a young couple on the other side of the road. There's bad blood between their families. And, unfortunately, the plant hit Madame la Maire."

Yann continued, "But there is a bigger problem in Louennec. Seznec is part of a group of far-right nationalists who are stirring up anti-foreign sentiments. We are keeping an eye on them."

"You mean that Meredith might have been targeted because she's English?" Pippa said, her voice hushed. "I mean, she's got French citizenship of course, but everyone thinks of her as English."

"Maybe, maybe not," said Yann. "You may remember an earlier incident at her property."

Pippa nodded. Meredith's garage had been spray-painted with the words *Rosbifs Go Home* when she was running for mayor.

"Who would want to hurt Meredith though?"

Yann put a finger to his lips. "You must be discreet, Peeper. I can think of the *secrétaire de la mairie*, for example, who we believe is part of that extremist *mouvance*."

"Really? Sylvie Le Goff?" Pippa put her hand to her mouth, knocking over her glass of wine. The waiter rushed over to wipe it up, and brought her another glass on the house.

"You know how it is in these rural communities," Yann said when the waiter had gone. "The extreme right is relatively new in Finistère, but we also have the extreme left — the eco-terrorists, we call them — and the two groups hate each other." He sighed. "*C'est un panier de crabes*. They get upset about the smallest things and violence breaks out."

"And we get caught in the middle. I wonder which side the metalheads are on," she mused. "You saw them at the funeral procession."

He smiled. "You're a smart woman. I'm sorry to say that when Rockface moved here, he drew extremists to Louennec. There are now at least two heavy metal festivals in the region every year. It attracts *les marginaux*, you understand, people who don't fit in; they are macho and working class, many of them. And they have grievances."

"Are you saying all those fans dressed in black are far right? I can't believe it."

"It depends. It's complicated," he said. "You can ask Rockface's widow. But did you notice that his old songs were the most popular, the ones with the typical black metal themes of extreme violence, including references to Nazism?"

Pippa shook her head. "I'm afraid I never saw any of his concerts — hard rock isn't really my thing. Although I now know he bit the heads off chickens when he performed," she said. Yann looked alarmed.

"But the eco-activists are the most prevalent in Brittany, aren't they?" she added.

"That is the problem," he replied. "We have a long history of nationalism here in Brittany. But, also, there are feuds between village families that have been going on for years, generations even. Take Tanguy Seznec, for example. He is at war with the Charpentiers. They were his target on the day of the funeral. Their parents expropriated his family from their home in Louennec, which is why the Seznecs live in Kerivac. Sometimes it gets violent. But what are we expected to do?"

"And what about Alex? Are you any closer to finding his killer?" she asked.

"Any closer? I'm afraid not. As you know, the murder weapon can't be traced to any of the hunters . . . and do you have any idea how many unauthorised guns there are in the *commune*?"

He took his wallet from his jeans pocket. "Shall we get the bill?"

CHAPTER 22

Balanced on a pair of crutches, Prue waited on the railway platform while Jonathan heaved her luggage onto the train. Jennifer watched. She wasn't going to let that aqua-coloured suitcase ambush her a second time.

Her mother-in-law grudgingly accepted her goodbye kiss. "Well, goodbye," said Prue. "I'll be glad to get back to some decent food after the disgusting mess they served at that rehab place."

Jennifer said nothing. She was counting the minutes until her mother-in-law finally departed. Jonathan went on board to help settle Prue in her first-class seat. Jennifer watched him make her comfortable and check she had her book, a bottle of water and a homemade baguette sandwich on the table in front of her.

She turned and waved to Jennifer just as Jonathan stepped off the train. He blew his mother a kiss.

The ordeal was over.

"It would be easier if she wasn't so ungrateful," Jennifer commented as they left the platform. Jonathan merely grunted. Jennifer wondered whether he still blamed her for the accident. Wasn't he ever going to thank her for having Prue to stay in the first place? She nursed her resentment in silence.

"So, Blackie finally had her lambs," he remarked.

"Yes. It was very exciting. Luke was in his element."

"He told me all about it. Everything else OK?"

"Fine, thanks. You?"

He nodded. They reached their cars. About to climb into his Volvo, he said, "I hear you've got some help on the farm."

"And who told you that?" she said, before realising that it must have been Luke. "And? What of it?"

"Oh, nothing." He got into the car and rolled down the window. "What's his name, your cheesemonger?"

Jennifer bristled at his patronising tone. What business was it of his who she was seeing?

She scowled. "If you must know, it's Philippe."

"So, Saturday as usual? I'll pick them up," he said, driving off with a wave, which she ignored. Another round to Jonathan.

Jennifer opened her car door, her stomach clenched with stress. She checked her phone and realised it was already time to pick up the children. Mariam would be first today, as her school was in town. She was outside, waiting, when Jennifer pulled up.

"Had a good day?" Jennifer asked.

Mariam seemed unusually cheerful. Jennifer watched her daughter's gaze follow two boys walking along the pavement. Could one of them be . . . ?

They took the short cut back to Louennec across the river, Jennifer wondering how to broach the issue. It was bound to happen at some point. Even Prue had asked her if Mariam had a boyfriend. What if she'd been right?

They reached Luke's school and he jumped into the back. Mariam was texting on her phone, increasing Jennifer's suspicion.

Byron was sitting outside waiting for them when they got home. Luke went off to see the rabbits, while Mariam pushed past the dog and headed for the stairs. After a moment's hesitation, Jennifer followed her up.

Mariam's bedroom door was ajar. Jennifer saw her at her desk, looking out over the front garden. Greta Thunberg scowled at them from a wall poster.

"Mariam," Jennifer began, "don't you think thirteen is a bit young to have a boyfriend?"

Mariam turned round and stared at her mother. "What are you talking about?"

Jennifer plunged on. "You know perfectly well what I mean. Who were those two boys you were looking at when I picked you up?"

Mariam took her time to respond. "You mean Eric and his friend? He's Pervenche's boyfriend."

Jennifer felt her cheeks grow warm, a mixture of relief and embarrassment. "It's not that I don't want you to have a boyfriend, you know that. It's just . . . you know. What's the rush? You've plenty of time."

They stared at each other in silence. Jennifer had no idea how to broach the issue of sex. She ended up saying, "Anyway, you know you can talk to me, don't you?"

Mariam nodded and turned away. Jennifer suddenly remembered that in her concern for Mariam, she'd forgotten to pick up a baguette on the way home.

"I'm going to Pippa's for some bread," she said at the door. "You can come with me if you like."

The suggestion was met with silence. As she drove along the lanes back to Louennec, Jennifer pondered those conversations she needed to have with her daughter. The prospect made her toes curl. Wasn't the school supposed to be responsible for sex education these days? She parked the car outside the *mairie* and crossed the street to the bakery, where she found Pippa deep in conversation with Vicky.

"Hi!" she said. "What's up?"

Vicky turned round. "We were just talking about Alex's missing motorbike."

"Are you sure he didn't sell it before he died?" Jennifer asked.

Vicky shook her head. "I've been going through his papers, and so far there's no sign of any transaction like that. But the study's in a terrible mess, there's piles of paper covered in his scribbles everywhere."

She sighed. "I'm assuming it was stolen. Let's face it, from what Derek was saying, it would be worth someone's while to take it."

"I suppose so," said Jennifer. "Had the barn been broken into?"

"Nope. That's the point. It must have been someone with a key. And that means it was someone on my staff."

CHAPTER 23

At the village hall they were celebrating the *fest-noz*, the first Saturday night in May. The reedy sound of the *biniou*, the Breton bagpipe, reached the people queuing outside to get in.

The woman at the door waved Luke and Mariam through, but apologetically charged Jennifer six euros. The kids joined their schoolfriends who stood grouped at each side of the hall, Jennifer having warned them, with a tap on her watch, that they'd be leaving at nine thirty sharp.

The room was crowded with people of all ages. Before Jennifer could even look round, Philippe was at her side. To her the *fest-noz* felt like a coming out, a public acknowledgement that she and Philippe were a couple. Why should she care? The whole village probably knew anyway. They were all here tonight, from the butcher to the vet.

"Isn't this nice?" said Meredith, joining them. A small group of singers had gathered at the front and began intoning a Breton chant, each one with a hand pinned to their ear.

"There'll be dancing in a bit," Meredith added, raising her long gypsy skirt as though ready to roll.

"How's it going?" Jennifer asked, noticing her buoyant mood. "It looks like your gout is a lot better."

Meredith smiled. "I've kept my cane, just in case," she said. "All's going well, actually. Jean-Michel showed a representative of the *département* round the village today to discuss our plans for the France in Bloom contest. We're about to start laying a cycling path along the river as part of our village improvements. But, you'll never guess what I heard today." She almost jumped up and down in her excitement. "The Tour de France will be coming through Carhaix just before the Vieilles Charrues, and it will pass along the main road outside Louennec!"

Philippe raised his glass. "This is amazing," he said. "The Tour has never come here before."

"Wow," said Jennifer. "Luke will be thrilled. That's great publicity, well done, Meredith."

"Oh, it's nothing to do with me," Meredith said. "It just happens to be coming through central Brittany this year." She turned and waved to Vicky, who was just then entering the hall, Pierre steering her with a hand at her elbow.

"Oh look!" said Jennifer. "Is that Sylvie Le Goff over there? Isn't she the one who kicked up rough over the flower competition?"

Scanning the room, Meredith spotted the small, thin woman with a tight face talking to a couple of youngish villagers by the *buvette*. Both were dressed in the trademark black of the heavy metal fans who'd lined the streets on the day of Alex's funeral. Following Meredith's gaze, Jennifer saw one of them with a ponytail and ugly nose ring look at Mariam and say something to Sylvie with a sneer. Sylvie looked across at Jennifer, who returned the stare. She felt like going over and slapping the man in the face.

Meredith grimaced. "Yes, that's her. She's already going through the accounts to make sure I don't start spending money that we don't have on the project. But it's not costing us much anyway. And she needs to think of the benefits for everyone."

At that moment, an accordionist got up and played a few chords. A trim woman in her thirties, her hair tied back, stepped to the front and introduced herself as the head of the traditional dancing association and their teacher for the evening. She explained that they'd be doing Breton, Irish and Scottish dancing.

Amid some confusion, all those present gathered into two groups, and each formed a circle. Jennifer beckoned to Mariam and Luke who came over to join their group. Philippe took Mariam's hand, which she surrendered grudgingly, and reached out for Jennifer with the other. Pippa pushed in and stood next to Luke. As Jennifer looked across the ring, she saw Jonathan and Emma facing her on the opposite side. She acknowledged Jonathan, who was looking pointedly at her, with a tense smile. His eyes slid across to Philippe and he smiled knowingly.

"Where's Yann?" Jennifer asked Pippa. "Didn't he get the night off?"

Pippa grimaced. "He's monitoring another urban rodeo in town. Haven't young people got anything better to do? They could be here, enjoying themselves doing traditional dancing."

Never having been to a *fest-noz* before, Jennifer had no idea what she was supposed to do. The only thing she did know was that the back and forth of the steps kept bringing her into eye contact with Jonathan on the opposite side of the circle. Though she averted her gaze, she could feel Emma staring at her.

Gradually, above the music and the heavy stamp of feet, the sound of raised voices could be heard coming from the second circle. The members of this group, Sylvie Le Goff among them, seemed to be calling out disparaging remarks. It was hard to make out exactly what they were shouting, but during a pause in the music, she heard a reference to "Madame la Maire", followed by laughter. She glanced at Meredith who, thankfully, was happily twirling with a partner.

But Jean-Michel had heard, all right. Every single word. Jennifer kept an eye on him as, instructed by their teacher, the two groups lined up facing each other. She noticed that most of the men in Sylvie Le Goff's circle were dressed in ripped jeans, boots and camouflage trousers.

To a jolly tune from the accordion, the two lines moved towards each other. As soon as Jean-Michel was within touching distance of the man opposite, he punched him on the nose. A young couple from Jennifer's line broke away, pointing at the victim, who retaliated by kicking Jean-Michel in the gut. He bent over, winded. Sylvie Le Goff watched in silence from her place in her line, lips twisted in a sardonic smile.

Following this encounter, a generalised scuffle broke out between the two lines. Jennifer dropped Philippe's hand and looked around for the children, who had promptly disappeared. Meredith, in her role as mayor, held up a hand and tried to call for order. Nobody listened.

With no idea why they were fighting, Jennifer was momentarily reminded of the Sharks against the Jets in *West Side Story* as the music played on.

"Do something!" she said to Philippe. But, like everyone else, he was glued to the spot, staring at the combatants as though mesmerised. By now, Jean-Michel's shirt was spattered with blood.

The music stopped, while the dance teacher stood with her hands over her mouth. It was Vicky who eventually stepped in. She grabbed Jean-Michel's attacker by his ponytail and shouted at him, "Ca *suffit!*"

A guilty silence descended on the dancers, who stood looking at each other, embarrassed and bemused. Whatever had happened to their peaceful little village?

Meredith climbed on to the stage. "I think we'd better all go home and cool off."

The guy with the ponytail, blood dripping from his nose ring, stood to one side, surrounded by his metalhead pals.

Jean-Michel, assisted by a friend, made his way to the Gents to tend to his wounds. Luke and Mariam materialised from nowhere and stood with Jennifer. She looked around for Pippa, who was nowhere to be seen.

"We're going," Jennifer said to Philippe.

On their way out, they ran into Vicky.

"How did you manage to stop the fight?" Jennifer asked. "Did you know that man with the ponytail?"

"Easy," Vicky replied. "It's Tanguy Seznec, our handyman. I'm seeing him and the rest of the staff about the stolen motorbike tomorrow. He'd better be on his best behaviour."

She added, "My gardener was there too actually, in our line. Erwan. I should have introduced you. He might be interested in helping you out. He and Tanguy can't stand each other, God knows why."

"Did you say Seznec?" Jennifer asked. She remembered the girl who had bullied Mariam during the previous school year. She had driven over to their village to read the riot act to the mother, a hatchet-faced woman called Madame Seznec. She had informed Madame Seznec that she never wanted to see her at her market stall again. Had the entire Seznec family been at the *fest-noz*?

"He's the father of the girl who bullied Mariam last year!" she exclaimed.

CHAPTER 24

Vicky had installed herself at the dining-room table, looking out through the window. The sweeping view over the lawn and the flowerbeds was veiled with a fine mist of drizzle. The roses, which were about to burst into bloom, had their heads bowed as if awaiting judgement. Vicky, a notebook in front of her, was ready to interview her staff. One of them had to know something about the missing motorbike.

First up was the cook, Bleuzenn, a stout woman in her early forties, born and bred in Louennec. Vicky liked and trusted her, largely because she was a fount of local gossip.

"I'm sorry for disturbing you on a Sunday," Vicky began, wishing, as always, that she spoke better French. They shook hands, and Bleuzenn sat down on the opposite side of the table with her back to the bay window. Normally the two women communicated in a mixture of basic words and gestures. But this wouldn't do for the present interview, so Vicky had downloaded a translation app onto her phone.

She opened the app and began. "I am seeing each one of you individually to ask you about an important matter that has arisen — the disappearance of a prize motorbike that belonged to Alex."

Hearing a stream of impeccable French, Bleuzenn stared at the phone and then back at Vicky. If she was going to talk into a phone, couldn't her boss have just rung her instead of calling her in on her day off? But at least she understood what Vicky was saying, for once.

Vicky held out the phone and pointed at it.

"I don't know anything about that, madame. Where was it?" said Bleuzenn.

"It was in the barn where he kept all his motorbikes. The barn hadn't been broken into, so the bike must have been stolen by somebody who had access to a key."

Bleuzenn brushed an imaginary speck of dust from her trousers and said she was scandalised that Madame could suggest that she, Bleuzenn, might be responsible for such a thing. "I don't know anything about motorbikes, madame. Why do you think it would be me?"

"Of course I'm not accusing you of stealing the bike. I'm just trying to establish what might have happened. I shall be interviewing all of you before I call the police."

"The police?" Bleuzenn blinked in alarm.

"Yes. The bike in question was worth a lot of money, in fact it was the most valuable one in the entire collection. That means it might have been stolen to order."

"I see." Bleuzenn frowned. "Well, if you ask me, you might be better off asking somebody who knows about motorbikes. Like Tanguy. He's got one, hasn't he?"

"Yes, he has. But just because he owns a motorbike it doesn't follow that he'd steal one, does it?"

Bleuzenn fell silent, waiting for the next question. It never came. Vicky asked her to let her know if she heard anything, and dismissed her. The subsequent interviews, with her two cleaning ladies and the gardener, followed the same pattern, concluding with each suggesting that the culprit must be Tanguy Seznec. Vicky began to wonder if they'd conspired to point the finger at him.

Finally, it was Tanguy's turn. He swaggered into the dining room in his usual black jeans and tank top under an open leather jacket. He gave no indication that he regretted his behaviour the previous night, indeed he seemed almost proud of it. Vicky had decided not to mention it. She gestured to the seat opposite and began with the same apology she'd given the others, for bringing him in on a Sunday morning. By now she was proficient in the app, which he seemed to find annoying.

Like the others, he professed his outrage at her implication that he might be a thief.

"But, Tanguy, it was someone who had a key. Apart from me, that means it was one of five people of whom you are one."

"You have no right to make such accusations!" he declared. "Rockface may have left the barn open because we needed the tools and the machinery. Did you ever check that he left it locked?"

She hadn't, but said nothing. She didn't dare mention that the others all accused him, and was still wondering whether his ownership of a motorbike was relevant. Weren't all metalheads bikers?

"What if Rockface sold it", Tanguy went on, "without telling you?"

Vicky had already thought of that possibility. She did wonder whether Alex had planned to surprise her by finally renovating the abandoned east wing. But she needed her employee to know that she was the boss. She'd only kept him on because Alex seemed to have a soft spot for him.

"I'm sorry, Tanguy, but I'm left with no option but to contact the gendarmerie," she said. "It was a vintage Brough, and whoever stole it knew that it was the most valuable bike in Alex's collection."

He got up with a dismissive "*pff*" and stalked out of the room without shaking hands.

* * *

Vicky swivelled round to look at the grandfather clock, and saw that it was about to chime midday. Alex had always

110

complained about that damned clock, which marked every quarter hour with a *bong* which made them jump every time.

Needing to get out of the house, she drove to Louennec and parked outside the bakery. Pippa was with a customer. While she waited for them to be served, Armel, the local dairy farmer who'd been in Alex's hunting party, wandered in. He took one look at the customer Pippa was serving and walked out, without even greeting Vicky. What was going on?

The customer left with a baguette and a rum baba.

"Did you see that?" Vicky asked Pippa, who rolled her eyes.

"Oh yes. It's one of those petty village rivalries. It goes back to the row over the wind farm project," Pippa explained. "Armel — who's on the council, by the way — got money from the developers for a substation. And some of the villagers who were opposed to the project haven't spoken to him since! I presume that was one of them." Pippa shrugged.

"My God, this place," said Vicky. "You should see my lot at the château. I'll have a *pain complet*, please. Sliced."

Pippa picked up the wholemeal loaf and took it to the machine. "How are you?" she asked over the juddering of the slicer.

"Could be better. I'm trying to get to the bottom of who stole Alex's motorbike. This morning, I called in all the staff — who deny it, of course, but I've got a creeping feeling that it might be Tanguy."

"Is that the same Tanguy who got in the fight with Jean-Michel last night at the *fest-noz*?"

Vicky nodded. "Yes. Tanguy Seznec."

"So, he's your handyman? I didn't realise that. I hear that he might be involved with the extreme right," said Pippa. "In fact, I understand that it was him who threw the plant at Meredith in the funeral procession."

"You're effing kidding me!" Vicky said. "One of my own employees starts a riot at my husband's funeral! How could he do such a thing? Mind, I discovered today that none of my staff like Tanguy. I'm going to report him to the police. I mean it's a bit of a coincidence that he has a bike, innit?"

"Isn't that a little harsh?" Pippa ventured, but Vicky waved away her objection. "I know it's not relevant to the motorbike issue, but Yann tells me that extremists got more active after you and Alex moved here, I presume because of his reputation."

"You mean when he was biting the heads off chickens and so on? I'd say he was always the same old grumpy bastard," Vicky said with a smile. "And he never took politics, or himself, too seriously. He was an entertainer, that's it. Basically, his fans stuck with him. Right to the end he kept on performing the same old hits — minus the chicken biting."

She paid for her loaf and was turning to go when her phone rang. She listened to the caller for a moment, and then her face froze. She whispered, "Oh my God."

She rang off and leaned against the counter.

"What's happened?" Pippa asked.

Her voice trembling, she said, "That was Meredith. Pierre's been found dead in his garden. They think he might have topped himself. I've got to go there straight away."

CHAPTER 25

Pierre's cottage, down a leafy lane on the outskirts of Louennec, was a white stucco, foursquare building with a granite-trimmed window on each side of the front door. A red ambulance stood outside, a gendarmerie vehicle parked nearby.

Vicky got out of her car just as the ambulance drove away. She saw that the path leading round the side of the building to the garden had been closed off with police tape. She swallowed. It was only a couple of evenings ago that she and Pierre had enjoyed drinks on the terrace back there.

A woman, dressed in the pale blue polo shirt and dark trousers of a gendarme, came round the corner and ducked under the tape. Vicky noticed that she had a gun tucked in a holster at her waist.

"*Maguy Gallou, maréchal des logis-chef, madame.*"

Vicky, suddenly unsteady, leaned against her car.

"I am Pierre Lambert's partner, Vicky Johnson. The mayor rang to tell me he has died. What happened?"

Pierre had been hit in the head by a ball, the gendarme said. What? How could that have killed him? Had he been playing football in the garden? Seeing that Vicky was having difficulty understanding, the gendarme repeated, "*Une balle dans la tête,*" and pointed two fingers at her own head.

"Shot?" Vicky said in English. The gendarme nodded. "Where?"

"At the bottom of the garden," the officer said in English. "The neighbour heard the sound and found him."

Vicky took a step towards the police tape, but the gendarme held her back.

"Please, madame. We must leave the scene untouched. Madame la Maire has just left, and the prosecutor will be here soon."

This is too much to bear, she thought. *First Alex, now this.* She swayed, the gendarme catching her just before she fell. She got into the car, sat in the driving seat and burst into tears.

Another gendarme, tall and slim with a shaven head, appeared behind the policewoman. "*Adjudant-chef Yann Berthou,*" he said. The name sounded familiar somehow. He shook her hand warmly and said, in French, then translated by his colleague, "I am Pippa's friend. I'm sorry we have to meet in such sad circumstances, but thank you for coming. You received the phone call from Meredith? We called her to confirm the death in her role as mayor."

"Yes." She opened the glove box and felt around for tissues.

"The gendarmerie also asked the mayor to contact you because we have the record of the interview we had with you and Monsieur Lambert after your husband died in March," Yann said. Vicky remembered only too well the accusation that she and Pierre may have conspired to murder Alex, and she stiffened.

"Do you know who is his next of kin?" Yann asked.

Vicky blew her nose loudly. "No. He's never mentioned any children, and I believe his parents have passed away . . . Did he shoot himself, or what?" she asked Yann.

He shrugged. "Maybe, maybe not. That's what we will have to establish. The coroner has ordered an autopsy. We're hoping you can help us. The investigators will be in touch with you."

"What do you need to know?"

"Well, for example, did he have any problems that might have caused him to want to end his life?"

"Only that your drone spotted that he was growing cannabis," she said. She hadn't meant to sound angry, but it came out that way. The two gendarmes glanced at each other.

"But I wouldn't say that made him want to commit suicide," she said. She remembered Pierre expressing the hope that he might get away with a fine or a suspended sentence since it was a first offence.

"Suppose it wasn't suicide?" she asked.

"He had a gun in his hand," Yann said. "The autopsy and forensics may give us more precise information about what happened. Is there anything else you can shed light on? Do you know of anyone who might want to harm him?"

Vicky shook her head. "I haven't the faintest idea. Oh, and while we're at it, I'm still waiting for your investigators to tell me who shot my husband. It's been two months now. Everyone in the village says hunting accidents happen so often that you lot don't investigate properly." The female police officer wandered off to the back garden, leaving Yann to deal with this troublesome woman.

Vicky switched on the engine. Yann bent down to the car window and said quietly and deliberately in French, "Madame, do you know how many unauthorised guns there are in people's possession around Carhaix? We have established that none of your husband's friends fired the fatal shot in the boar hunt. We are continuing our investigation, I can assure you, but it will take time.

"Do you understand?" he added, frowning.

Slightly shamefaced, Vicky asked, "Did you find any clues inside Pierre's house?"

Yann glanced over his shoulder and said slowly, in English, "It seems Monsieur Lambert died before finishing his lunch."

CHAPTER 26

Hearing a knock on her office door, Meredith looked up to see a sheepish-looking Jean-Michel standing in the entrance.

"I'm sorry about Saturday night," he began, "*mais c'était insupportable!*"

"Please, sit down and explain." She paused as he pulled up a plastic chair to the enormous oak desk she'd inherited from her predecessor, then added, "It was terribly embarrassing."

"I wasn't just going to stand there and let them complain about our flower campaign. I felt responsible because I was the one who drew up the application—"

"Yes, but it's me who's responsible for the campaign," she said.

"But that's the point, Meredith. They were insulting you!"

"And who was that young couple who joined you when the fighting broke out?"

"Ah, the Charpentiers. They are the villagers who filmed the *terroristes* destroying their flowerbeds."

"I see." Meredith recalled the video recording they had been shown at a council meeting. "And so they suspected that the two young men with Sylvie were the perpetrators—"

"Yes, although I don't know whether it really was them," said Jean-Michel with a shrug. "The Charpentiers can't stand the Seznecs, and vice versa, because of some stupid family property dispute going back to when their parents were alive. All it takes is an excuse and it blows up again. I was defending the Charpentiers, of course, because they are my neighbours."

"The question is, do we think Sylvie is behind this . . . this civil disobedience?"

"She could be," said Jean-Michel, "but how do we prove it?"

"I've had just about enough of that damned woman!" Meredith cried. "She's toxic! And so petty. Every time I come up with some new initiative, she says, 'That's not how we do things around here.' Anyone would think it's she who is the mayor." Meredith ruminated for a moment, and then her face lit up. "Can I fire her?"

Jean-Michel looked dubious. "She's a public official. She'd fight it, and hard. You could try, but I don't think you'd get anywhere."

Meredith sighed. "Anyway, that's not why I wanted to see you. It's about the France in Bloom competition. How did it go on Saturday? What did the representative from Quimper have to say about our plans?"

Jean-Michel spread his hands. "On the positive side, he told me that for our first star, we probably won't need the regional committee to come and inspect us. As we're a *commune* of less than a thousand people, we can probably just submit photos with the application and they'll base their decision on those."

"That's good news," Meredith said.

"The first half of the visit went fine. I showed him where we'd thought of planting cherry trees, and then took him for a walk by the river. He liked our decision to position the benches near the willows for shade, and agreed that the cycle path should be wide enough for pedestrians to walk two abreast. He really liked the idea of asking the schoolchildren to draw signs along the path, like we discussed."

He cleared his throat. "But then, on our way back into the village, he unfortunately noticed the flowerbeds that had been torn up. Maybe I should have made up some story to explain it, but I couldn't think of anything, so I, er, admitted that our application didn't have the support of the whole village."

Meredith frowned. "Hmm. I'm not sure that was a good idea. You could have said the homeowners were about to start planting, or something."

"The trouble is, he'd seen a story in *Le Télégramme* dating from Alex's funeral, which mentioned that some residents are against our application. So, it's just as well I didn't try to cover it up. I told him that we were getting the villagers on side and that everything will be fine. Oh, and he liked the hedgehog tunnels."

Their eyes met across the desk. Each knew what the other was thinking. And it wasn't good. With the village now divided into two opposing camps, how would they get everyone on side in time?

Jean-Michel was at the door when Meredith asked him:

"Did you hear the news about Pierre Lambert? He's dead. I had the difficult task of breaking it to Vicky Johnson. The gendarmerie seems to think he killed himself."

"Yes, I did know," he said. "Tragic, isn't it? Pierre and I were with Rockface when he was shot, and now he's dead too. I heard he was in some sort of trouble, but to commit suicide? He just wasn't the type."

CHAPTER 27

Jennifer was bent double, picking Gariguette strawberries in the vegetable patch when she heard the purr of Jonathan's Volvo on the track beside the fence.

She stood up and stretched. In any case it was time to get ready for the market. Having fed the animals and collected the eggs, she felt like she'd already done a day's work.

Jonathan strolled over to her.

"How's it going?" he asked, sounding quite pleasant. Usually, they barely spoke when he came to collect the children.

"As you see," she said, suddenly resentful. "It's peak Gariguette season. Anyway, the kids are waiting. What are you going to do today?"

"It's a nice day, I thought I'd take them to the seaside."

She wrinkled her nose. "Well please don't take them to any of those stinking beaches with the killer seaweed. I had to cover a Greenpeace demonstration the other day; they'd dumped some outside the prefecture. God, did it stink!"

"Of course I won't," he said. "Who do you think I am?"

She shrugged. "I'm just saying. People have died from the stuff."

"Oh, stop exaggerating," he retorted.

"I'm not! It gets worse every year, what with the toxic runoff. Though what can you expect in a place which has more pigs than people living in it?" She turned to go, before the exchange turned into a full-on row. "Anyway, I'd better get ready for market."

"Look, we need to talk."

Jennifer glanced at him. He sounded different somehow.

"Not today. I'm busy, in case you hadn't noticed." She could see he was hurt, and felt a bit guilty. "How's your mother, by the way?"

But he wasn't so easily placated. "She's fine. I wondered when you'd bother to ask."

She returned to her strawberries and began putting the fruit into punnets. When, a few minutes later, she came back with a crateful, Luke and Mariam were getting into the car, Jonathan putting their beach things into the boot. Mariam was in her own little world, cut off by the earbuds Jonathan had given her for Christmas. Maybe she still blamed Jonathan for leaving them, or maybe she was fed up with going everywhere with her little brother, now that she was growing up. Jennifer felt a prick of sympathy for her.

She packed her own car with her market produce, along with some cheerful ranunculi which Mariam had tied into bunches. As she drove past the fields of newly sprouting corn and pale green wheat rippling in the breeze, she wondered what Jonathan had wanted to talk about. The summer holidays, perhaps, the first they'd be spending apart. July wouldn't be a problem, as the kids would probably want to stay for the Vieilles Charrues festival and the Tour de France, but what about August? She could imagine Luke going away with Jonathan, Emma and Romy, who was in his class. But what of Mariam? She wouldn't want to join them. And now that her friend Pervenche was *en couple* — which, according to the mothers at the school gates meant nothing more than hand-holding and snogging — Mariam might not be invited to spend the summer holiday with her. Still, it was only spring; there was plenty of time to work something out.

When Jennifer arrived, Pippa was already at her new stall and serving customers. A sign announcing *Artisan Boulanger* was draped across the front of the table. She'd set up her stall having noticed that a rival bakery had opened one in the market. "If you can't beat them, join them," she'd said. Jennifer watched Pippa greeting her regular customers, who were lining up to buy her loaves, cakes and sausage rolls. Sensing Philippe's eyes on her from his cheese stall across the way, she gave him a smile.

There was an awkward moment when Emma strolled into view, followed by Romy, who kept trying to drag her mother towards the cheap dress stalls along the back. Emma gave Jennifer a wide berth, but as she was within hearing distance, Jennifer said loudly to Pippa, "There's a lot of hornets around this year, don't you find?"

Pippa smiled. "Yes, they're hard to get rid of."

Emma wandered over to Philippe's stall where he cut her a large slice of Brie. Jennifer couldn't help feeling uneasy. For goodness' sake, she told herself, why shouldn't Emma buy cheese? Despite Emma's presence, Jennifer was relieved that there was no danger of running into Jonathan. The fact that he was with the children meant that she could spend the afternoon with Philippe, who'd offered to help out again with the gardening.

When the market closed for the day, Pippa and Jennifer repaired to the Central Café, where they made their way to their favourite table in the corner. Philippe and Jean-Luc, the crêpe-seller, were standing at the bar nursing glasses of red wine. The smell of Jean-Luc's *galettes saucisses* wafting in her direction from his stall had made Jennifer's mouth water.

"How does it feel to be back?" she asked Pippa.

"Great. Much better than the old days." Pippa grinned. "I can't believe I spent all that time struggling to get the Bretons interested in curry. I noticed that someone else has had the same idea."

Jennifer nodded. "You mean the Patels? You see, you were a trailblazer! And don't forget that's where you built up your customer base for when you opened the bakery."

They called out their orders for coffee to the waiter, who was busy behind the bar.

"It feels just like old times, doesn't it?" said Jennifer. "I guess Gwen is running the bakery this morning?"

"Yes. I'll be going over after this. But I'm actually thinking about taking on a part-time helper. It's getting really busy these days, what with our catering jobs as well."

"Ca te coutera la peau des fesses," said Jennifer, tapping her buttocks. They both laughed.

"I've just had a thought," Jennifer said after a while. "You've got daughters, right?"

Pippa looked at her quizzically. "Yes. Why?"

"Do you remember when they got interested in sex?"

Pippa laughed. "It was so long ago, I've almost forgotten all that. Joanne is doing her finals at university now and her sister is nineteen. Why do you want to know?"

"I've got a feeling that Mariam might have a boyfriend — one of her friends has. She denies it of course, and I've no reason to disbelieve her. She's only thirteen, after all."

"I'm sure it's perfectly innocent, if that's what you mean," said Pippa, patting her hand. "Wait till she gets to fifteen! You might well end up watching *Sex Education* on Netflix together."

"God forbid!" They both giggled. "Do you remember watching the telly with your parents when you were a kid, and a sex scene came on? I used to die from embarrassment."

"Oh yes. Though, of course they were so ancient they never had sex—"

"Whereas they were probably only forty, which is the age we are now." They grinned at each other, pausing while the waiter brought their drinks to the table. They sipped their coffees in silence for a while.

"Have you seen Vicky recently?" Jennifer asked.

"Yes, I spent yesterday evening at her place. I feel terrible about Pierre. I don't know why I suspected he might have been involved in Alex's shooting." Pippa grimaced.

"His death would seem to rule him out, wouldn't it?" said Jennifer. "Unless you're a conspiracy theorist. But nobody seems to believe that he actually killed himself."

"Yann told Vicky that he never finished his lunch," said Pippa. "It's odd, that. It would indicate that somebody interrupted him. Vicky said she didn't understand the significance straight away. She thought he meant that a Frenchman would always finish his meal before topping himself, not that somebody had interrupted him."

"Really?" Jennifer laughed. "But if it was murder, who would want to kill Pierre? Could it be someone who was mad about him having it off with Vicky? Isn't jealousy one of the main motives for murder?"

"Or revenge," said Pippa. "Or money, I suppose. But in his case, he must have been worried about losing a source of income after the cops discovered his cannabis crop. That could have been a reason for killing himself."

Jennifer frowned. "I wonder about that guy Tanguy Seznec's role in all this."

"You mean he might have killed Pierre? Why?"

"How would I know?" Jennifer said. "I'm just thinking aloud. Look how he behaved at the *fest-noz* the other night. I mean, he's vicious, isn't he?"

"Just because he's a nasty bastard doesn't mean he's a killer. Come on. That theory sounds a little bit too convenient to me. Who knows, he might have been mates with Pierre. They're both locals."

"Well, for starters, we could ask Vicky if Tanguy was at the château on the day Alex was killed," Jennifer went on. "He's the father of the girl who called Mariam names at school last year. His wife is ghastly."

"Yann says Tanguy Seznec is a far-right sympathiser. He's also got a feud going on with one of the families in Louennec."

Jennifer frowned. "The extreme right stirring things up here makes me very uneasy — because of Mariam. I feel like I should be protecting her from racism. She's already vulnerable, having been abandoned twice — first by her birth mother and now by Jonathan. If the extreme right gets a foothold here, I'd be worried about the impact on her. Look what happened at Alex's funeral. It's like battle lines are being drawn."

"Vicky's obviously got it in for Seznec," said Pippa. "She reported him to the police over the theft of Alex's prize motor-bike. We'll have to wait and see what that throws up."

CHAPTER 28

Market day was also Pippa's turn to make dinner for Yann.

It was warm outside, so she opened the French windows on to the patio while she diced vegetables for a spicy Thai stir-fry with a peanut sauce and rice. The doorbell rang when it was all ready to be heated up.

Yann was an appreciative dinner guest and always complimented her on her cooking, even though she'd only had time to concoct something quickly. She knew that he enjoyed cooking, which made her rather ashamed of her limited culinary range. Here in Louennec, the option of home delivery wasn't available, unlike in London where she'd relied on them when she had no time to cook.

She invited Yann out to the patio, a mirror image of his, and poured them both a glass of Gros Plant. He helped himself to crisps from a bowl and leaned back with a contented sigh, surveying her small rectangle of lawn with its border of low-maintenance perennials.

"How's work?" she asked.

He smiled. "You know that if I tell you what I'm doing, I have to kill you."

Pippa was undeterred. "I hear that Vicky has made a complaint about Tanguy Seznec."

"Aha, the motorbike theft. Indeed she did."

"Vicky said it has to be someone with a key. Which means that the guy is the prime suspect, doesn't it?"

Yann tilted his head to the side. "Maybe, maybe not," his habitual non-committal response which never failed to irritate her.

She stood up and went into the kitchen. Yann followed her, carrying the empty crisp bowl, and stood watching her put the frying pan on the hob. Cubes of chicken were waiting in the fridge to be thrown in with spices.

"What I'm saying, Peeper, is that even if he is the prime suspect, what's the motive? We don't know that he had anything against his employer. We believe they were friends. Why would he want to hurt him by stealing his motorbike like that? He already had one of his own. Unless he needed the money, of course. And in any case we'd need proof."

Pippa concentrated on sliding chopped onion into hot oil and waiting for it to soften. She dropped in the chicken pieces and turned back to face him.

"But don't you think he's the most likely member of Vicky's staff to have taken it?"

"What are you saying? That we should arrest him because she says so? If we did that, half of the French population would be in jail." He harrumphed. "The investigators will have to interview all the potential suspects, not just the one whose boss thinks he's the thief."

Pippa knew he was right. But she added, "I know something else about Seznec which might be of interest to you."

Yann shot her one of his piercing looks. "Jennifer", Pippa went on, "told me that Seznec's daughter was bullying hers and calling her names."

"Jennifer's daughter from Somalia?" Yann drew up a chair at the kitchen table and sat stroking his chin.

"Yes! They're racists obviously. You remember you told me that he supports the extreme right, or is a sympathiser at least. He was at the *fest-noz* in Louennec the other night and got into a fight. It all fits, doesn't it?"

"That's possible," said Yann. He put a finger to his lips. "But we are interested in Seznec in connection with another matter. The examining magistrate is issuing a search warrant for his property."

"A search warrant?"

Yann nodded. "Shall I set the table?"

Pippa pulled out cutlery from a kitchen drawer and handed them to Yann. She threw the chopped vegetables into the pan and stirred the mixture, while keeping an eye on the rice which was almost ready.

"Is red OK with this?" she asked him. "Do you mind opening a bottle?"

He disappeared into the living room and returned with a bottle of Côtes du Rhône. "Is this what you had in mind?"

"Perfect."

Pippa served the food onto plates warmed in the microwave, which Yann always found amusing, and waited for his verdict.

"Delicious," he said, closing his eyes.

"It's only a stir-fry," she said. "It's simple."

"I wouldn't know where to start," he said. "All I know is French cuisine."

Pippa returned to the subject of Tanguy Seznec. "So, why do you want to search his place?"

"We suspect him of being one of the ringleaders of the extremists who have been causing so much trouble in the village. We may find evidence at his house or on his devices. Of course, during the search we may also find incriminating evidence regarding the stolen motorbike."

"What do you mean?" She leaned forward, a forkful of food halfway to her mouth.

"Sometimes vintage motorbikes are sold to order. Or, if he's clever, he would have stripped it and sold the parts — more difficult to trace that way."

"And you'd be able to find the transactions on his phone or laptop or whatever?"

"Unless he was very careful and was doing the transactions in person, which of course is possible. We're talking about a lot of money. Anyway, we don't yet know if he's the culprit, do we?"

He eyed her thoughtfully while he ate. "You do know this is confidential, don't you, Peeper? You must be discreet. We cannot compromise the investigation."

She reached across the table and squeezed his hand.

"You can trust me," she said.

CHAPTER 29

Meredith, in a long flowing skirt, swept into the hall, where the other members of the council were waiting.

With a glance in Sylvie Le Goff's direction, she welcomed everyone to the meeting. Item number one on the agenda was the application for the Villes et Villages Fleuris competition.

"First, I believe you all know that a landscaping expert sent by the prefecture in Quimper came to have a look at our plans for the flower competition," she said. A few of those present began shuffling their papers.

"You already have the report, so I won't go into too much detail. The expert was shown the riverside path, and the sites for the rainwater collection tanks. The visit went well until, on his way back into the village, he noticed that some front gardens had had their plants pulled up."

Meredith sat up straighter and cast her eyes on the councillors. "Now, I have two things to say about this. The first is that we already have additional police patrols in Louennec because of a number of earlier disturbances that you are aware of. It would seem that, despite their presence, these incidents — which are clearly connected to the flower competition — have continued. I want you all to understand that this has to stop. It *must not* jeopardise our application."

"Second," she said, "many of you who were present at the *fest-noz* will have been as embarrassed as I was by the fist fight that broke out. It made me ashamed to be mayor, I can tell you. My understanding is that the fight was also linked to the flower competition, and highlighted once again the fact that the *commune* is not yet united behind the application."

She sighed. "I find it hard to comprehend why people would want to block this project. Far from doing harm, it will benefit the ecology, beautify our village and make it a more pleasant place to live in. It will also draw more tourists to the area." At her reference to the ecology, she noticed one of the farmers mutter something to his neighbour.

With a sidelong glance at Sylvie, she said, "It appears there are some people who may have another agenda in stirring up trouble in the village. If that is the case, I will ensure that the full force of the law is brought to bear on the miscreants. Having said that, I encourage all of you here today to help me promote our project among the villagers. We need to get everybody on side to win. Is that understood?"

Around the table, murmurs of "*Oui*" could be heard. Sylvie Le Goff, meanwhile, was busy shuffling her papers.

"Sylvie?"

The woman looked up, startled.

"I'll need an exact time frame from you as soon as possible, giving the dates when the trees are to be planted, and when we can expect the riverside path to be completed. I want to make sure everything that's needed has been ordered, and the expected delivery date, as well as the work schedule."

Sylvie scowled. She wasn't used to being told what to do.

"The point is that the stars are awarded to villages where the proposals have actually been implemented, not just set out on paper. In fact, if necessary, I may convene a public meeting so that we can bring the villagers up to speed and explain the importance of completing the work on schedule." Meredith sat back and looked around her.

Some of the members exchanged surprised glances. Sylvie pursed her lips as if to say, *This isn't how things are done here.*

"Any questions? Comments?" Meredith asked. Since nobody spoke, it was impossible to know if she had their unanimous support. She sighed, thinking, not for the first time, *No wonder they say France is ungovernable.*

"Well then, let's move on to point two of the agenda," she said. And they raced through the rest of the council business in record time.

Meredith wrapped up the meeting, waiting until everyone had left before collecting her things to depart. Jean-Michel was standing by the exit.

"That went well, I thought," he said. "It was a good idea to threaten them with a public meeting. You should have seen the look on Sylvie's face."

"I have resolved not to let her get away with it anymore," Meredith said. "I'm sick of being fobbed off. And it's now getting urgent. We must stick to a strict timetable or we'll never get our first flower. And it's only one star, as I keep on saying!"

* * *

Meredith made her way back to her converted farmhouse, where she'd arranged to meet Emma later that evening.

She wasn't sure what her daughter wanted, but wondered if she needed help with her store. Or possibly with Romy. Emma had a regular babysitter, so Meredith was off the hook as far as that was concerned. It suited her because her duties as mayor seemed to take up all her waking hours.

She was surprised to see Emma's Clio already parked outside the garage. As she drew up beside it, her collie ran out of his kennel to greet her, circling around her as if he were rounding her up.

"Captain! I'm not a sheep." She pointed to the kennel and waited until he'd slunk back inside before going to the front door.

Emma was in the kitchen pouring herself a drink. She was wearing tight jeans and a low-cut top. Meredith had never approved of her daughter's fashion choices, but there was nothing she could do about it now Emma was nearly thirty.

"Have you had dinner?" Meredith asked.

"Yes. I left Jonathan putting Romy to bed. What about you?"

"What do you think?" Meredith replied. "I've just got back from a council meeting. Now I know why your father got so frustrated with the damned thing, and he wasn't even mayor. That woman is just so disagreeable."

"You mean Sylvie Le Goff? Can't you get rid of her?"

Meredith grimaced. "Only in theory. No, I'm stuck with her, more's the pity. So, from now on, I'm going to try handling her in a different way, and make her actually do the job she's paid for, instead of trying to undermine me all the time. Anyway, never mind about me. What's going on with you?"

"Well, to be honest, things aren't going all that well with Jonathan, and I wondered if you might be able to take Romy for a weekend so that the two of us could go off somewhere and spend some time together."

Meredith appreciated her daughter's taste in men even less than her taste in clothes. She wasn't a big fan of Jonathan, who was at least ten years older than Emma, but she couldn't blame him, having seen how Emma had set out to attract him. She felt sorry for Jennifer, who'd become a loyal friend following Craig's sudden death.

"That didn't take long," Meredith said drily. "He only moved in a few months ago."

"Yes. And as you know, he's got his own childcare issues, which complicates things. But it's not that. Ever since he found out that Jennifer is seeing someone, he hasn't been the same somehow."

"You mean Philippe?" Meredith said. "Why shouldn't she be seeing him? I mean Jonathan was the one who left, wasn't he?"

"Wait a sec, just whose side are you on, Mum?"

"Yours of course, dear."

Meredith opened the fridge to see what she could find for her supper. Since Craig's death, she no longer felt obliged to cook meat and two veg in the evening. Now, she saw that she had the ingredients for a Greek salad: black olives, feta cheese, tomatoes, cucumber and a red onion.

"Come and sit with me," she said. She took a bottle of Gros Plant from the fridge and went into the living room in search of glasses. She sat down on the sofa and patted the cushion next to her. Emma sat, and mother and daughter stared into the imposing granite fireplace in silence for a while.

"How's everything else? I haven't seen you properly in ages," Meredith began. "And of course, I'll be happy to take Romy for a weekend. Just let me know when."

"Thanks, Mum. Well, I had a busy May — I've worked every single holiday except May Day. And now the weather's improving, the tourists are starting to arrive."

"I suppose you want to get away before July?"

Emma nodded. "That's the idea. July's always really busy because of the Vieilles Charrues. And we won't be going far. I'm thinking of heading for the Monts d'Arée and doing some hiking. Or maybe go to Morlaix and the coast."

"Sounds like a plan," said Meredith. "Well, like I said, just let me know."

Soon, Emma stood up, saying she'd let her mother get on with dinner. After seeing her to the door, Meredith returned to the kitchen where she began chopping her salad ingredients. She wasn't surprised to learn that Emma was having difficulties in her relationship. It was a pattern she'd observed over time, and she wondered whether it was really Jonathan who'd changed.

As she stirred the ingredients of a vinaigrette together in a salad bowl, Meredith realised she was caught in a dilemma. Of course she wanted her daughter to be happy, but she also cared about her friend Jennifer.

She shook her head sadly. After all, it was none of her business, was it?

CHAPTER 30

Jennifer pulled up outside the school gates, where Mariam and her new friend Ivy were deep in conversation. They were both in jeans, T-shirts and trainers.

Luke rolled down the window and yelled, "Mariam!" from the back of the car. Mariam muttered something to her friend, and the two of them laughed. No doubt she was complaining about her little brother. They strolled over to where Jennifer was holding up the traffic. A woman in the car behind her began sounding her horn.

"Mum, this is Ivy. Ivy — Mum," said Mariam, apparently oblivious to the traffic jam they'd caused. She got into the back with Luke, leaving Ivy to get in the front beside Jennifer, who therefore felt obliged to make conversation with her. Apart from the fact that Ivy was English, she was also the complete opposite of Pervenche. Whereas Mariam's French friend had a natural grace, a *je ne sais quoi*, Ivy was, well, loud. Her T-shirt was bright red, she shouted back to Mariam, and she appeared not to care that a roll of puppy fat hung over the top of her jeans. The two of them spent the entire journey home pulling apart each one of their teachers, and erupting in fits of giggles.

As soon as they got home, Mariam took Ivy to see the rabbits. Luke, subdued for once, went upstairs.

As usual, Byron was sitting in the way. Jennifer pushed past him into the kitchen and surveyed the contents of the fridge. Then hearing the girls come indoors, she said:

"As you probably know, Ivy, Mariam's vegan. What about you?"

"Oh, I'm fine, Jennifer," she said. "I eat anything." Jennifer didn't recall saying that she could address her by her first name but didn't see what she could do about it.

Jennifer decided to make a curry. Mariam could have veggies and the rest of them would share the remains of one of their broilers, which was already cooked.

The girls went upstairs, chattering away. She heard Luke slam his bedroom door. Half an hour later, they were seated around the kitchen table. It made a change to have an evening entirely in English, and a pleasure not to be subjected to the *verlan* that Mariam and Pervenche so annoyingly used.

By now the two girls had moved on to picking apart various classmates. Jennifer learned that a boy called Emeric was the class heartthrob, despite being lazy and stupid. They were especially derisory about a girl called Maelie, who'd been given detention for failing to do her homework.

"Did you say Maelie?" Jennifer asked. She put down her fork.

"Yes. Why?" Ivy asked.

"Oh, never mind," said Mariam, tossing her head. "She's the one I told you about."

Not wanting to reopen old wounds, Jennifer refrained from saying that Maelie was the girl who had bullied Mariam.

She brought out strawberries and ice cream for pudding. Luke was the first to finish his meal and pointed at the work rota. Jennifer had pinned it to the wall alongside the family photos — which included Jonathan. He was their father, after all.

"Mummy, it's my turn to shut the animals in," he announced, and got up without asking permission to leave the table. "I'm taking Byron."

"Just a moment," said Jennifer, annoyed at him for showing off. "I have to take Ivy home soon. Are you going to be all right here with Mariam?"

"Of course we are," Mariam said sulkily.

As soon as they'd finished their meal, Jennifer looked at her watch and realised it was getting late. Dusk was coming later now, and it was still daylight. She told Ivy it was time to go.

"See you tomorrow," Mariam said to her, and headed upstairs.

"So where do you live?" she asked Ivy as they got into the car.

"Kerivac."

"OK. That's where Maelie Seznec lives, isn't it?"

"Yeah. But we're not friends. She and her brother are always getting into trouble."

"What sort of trouble?" Jennifer asked.

"At school, mostly, like we were saying. The brother's as bad as her. He's a waste of space. I'll show you what I mean when we get to Kerivac," said Ivy.

Jennifer asked Ivy what her parents did. She said her father was an antiques dealer, and her mother worked at a supermarket in Carhaix, leaving Jennifer to wonder what sort of living they made.

They turned off the main road into Kerivac, which was less a village than a scattering of dwellings surrounding a patch of grass, which Jennifer assumed was supposed to be the village green. Two menhirs stood at one end. Jennifer remembered that the Seznec house was one of the first as you entered the hamlet. Ivy told her to stop in front of the megaliths.

"My place is just over there," she said, pointing to a modest white stuccoed house with a bank of pink hydrangeas outside. "I'll drop you there," Jennifer offered. "It's not much further."

"No. I'm fine. I wanted to show you this."

They got out of the car and Ivy walked across to the two megaliths.

"You see that?" she said. "Those two did it, the Seznec kids."

Jennifer got out and was stunned to read the protest message splashed across them in white paint: *NON au village fleuri!* The word *non* was written on one stone, the rest of the message on the other.

"That's awful!" said Jennifer. "How do you know it was them?"

"We saw them do it," Ivy replied.

CHAPTER 31

On a cloudless summer's day, Pippa, needing time to herself, set off for Kerivac. She went in search of artistic inspiration, and also to see for herself the vandalism Jennifer had described.

It was late afternoon on 21 June, the longest day, marked by the Fête de la Musique, a festival that was celebrated throughout France. She set off in the car to the strains of a clarinet coming from someone's open window.

A small concert was to take place outside the *mairie* in Louennec that evening. She left Gwen and her new part-time help at the bakery preparing sandwiches for a stall they planned to set up nearby. Luckily for Pippa, that year the summer solstice fell on a Monday, when the shop was closed to customers.

She had brought her easel and painting kit with her. Painting was the only thing that allowed her to relax, although she had very little time for it these days, what with the bakery and spending time with Yann. When she'd worked in London she'd at least been able to carve out time for herself at the weekend, and often went painting in Epping Forest, or the coast.

She parked the car on the grass verge at the entrance to Kerivac and walked to the two menhirs, where she stood shaking her head in dismay. Should she make a painting of them? What purpose would it serve? She wondered whether to paint the stones themselves, eliminating the hostile slogan, but that also seemed pointless.

She turned round and surveyed the hamlet. There was not a soul in sight. She spotted a hillock that would give her a view over the houses, with the menhirs in the background. She made her way along a path which led to an alleyway and the hill beyond. A couple of giant sycamore trees stood on the summit, their leaves trembling in the gentle breeze. It was only a short walk to the top where she set up her easel, looking down over the slate roofs of the houses below.

After about an hour, she'd worked out a composition centred on a spreading chestnut at the bottom of the hill. Now, she set about carefully painting the square, stuccoed houses.

Her tongue protruding slightly in concentration, she cast her eyes down to the street and caught sight of Jean-Michel's grey SUV approaching the menhirs. What was he doing here in office hours? Her interest piqued, she put down her brush and stood up to get a better view, just as the car disappeared into an alleyway behind the houses she was painting.

From where she stood, she had a clear view of a line of four ramshackle garages. Drifting up to her from below, she heard someone playing the first bars of "Für Elise" on a piano, repeated slowly, agonisingly. The sound reminded her that she ought to get back to Louennec, but first, she wanted to find out what Jean-Michel was up to.

She needed a closer look. She looked around for a better vantage point but there was none. So she raced down to the entrance to the row of garages, her heart pounding from the effort, where Jean-Michel had parked his car in the alleyway.

He had raised the door of the third garage along and was doing something at the back of the garage. Pippa could hear drawers being opened and shut, but could only make out the light of his phone torch dancing inside. He was whistling, intent on the task at hand.

She advanced cautiously behind a row of rubbish bins, craning her neck to see inside.

After a couple more minutes Jean-Michel, dressed in a smart suit, re-emerged from the shadows. Pippa stepped back and ducked down, but not before she had seen it. A motor-bike, standing at the front of the garage to one side, lit by the torch as Jean-Michel raised his arm to pull down the door.

CHAPTER 32

By the time Pippa got back to Louennec, Gwen had already set out the sandwiches and the *friands à la saucisse*. Their sausage rolls always sold well to the locals, who called them "so British".

"I'm so sorry, I got held up," Pippa said to her.

"*C'est pas grave, madame*," Gwen said with a smile. "*Tout va bien.*" Pippa dreaded the day when her assistant would move on to a better job in a bigger bakery. Meanwhile, she thanked her lucky stars once again that she had found such a hard-working and pleasant young woman to help her.

A small group of musicians had gathered in the little square, and Pippa heard the groan of the Breton bagpipe. People, drinks in hand, began trickling out of the bar-café opposite. Some began clapping in time to the music, and a couple of youngsters started to dance. Pippa left Gwen to sell the pastries, as she seemed to be enjoying chatting to the customers.

Yann, out of uniform, emerged from their cul-de-sac and kissed her on each cheek. Pippa could scarcely contain her excitement about what she'd seen, but instead she said, "Haven't you brought an instrument with you?"

He laughed. "I'm not musical. The only instrument I've ever played was the comb. What about you?"

"Wow, you mean where you put paper over the comb? We did that too when I was at school." She laughed. "I guess we're both more musical than we thought."

"Do you want to have dinner after this?" he asked. "It's a lovely evening."

"Sure. Although I ought to stay to the end to put everything away. I took some time off this afternoon to do some painting, and left Gwen doing all the work."

"Painting? Where did you go?"

Although she was burning to tell Yann, she was no longer certain that what she'd seen was *the* motorcycle.

"I was in Kerivac. There's a good view over the village and the menhirs from a hillock. Isn't it shocking that they've been vandalised like that?"

He frowned. "Yes. Terrible."

"I suppose you know that it was Tanguy Seznec's children who are most likely responsible?"

"Yes. Apparently. But as for the theft of Rockface's motorbike, we've found nothing to suggest Seznec had any connection to that."

"Oh." So much for that theory then. It suddenly struck her; what if Seznec and Jean-Michel had conspired to steal the motorbike? She wondered again whether to tell Yann what she'd seen that afternoon, but hesitated. She'd just had a better idea.

CHAPTER 33

Jennifer was on her way back to the house from the fishpond when she heard Jonathan's car approaching along the track.

The garden was in full bloom. She'd put up the faded yellow parasol so that Pippa could sit outside on a rather rickety chair and admire the gladioli and agapanthus flowering among the roses. Pippa had been enigmatic when she phoned, and wouldn't say why she wanted Jennifer to drive to Kerivac with her all of a sudden.

Jonathan hadn't called to say he was coming, and it wasn't his day to take the children, so she was puzzled as to the reason for this unannounced visit.

"Is something the matter?" she asked. "Come and take a seat. I'll bring out some lemonade."

When she re-emerged from the house with the drinks on a tray, he was sitting at the table, gazing mournfully at the garden. Byron was trailing behind Jennifer, and Jonathan called to him, bent down and buried his face in his fur. Byron looked startled. He clearly hadn't expected this behaviour from his master.

"Want some?" Jennifer asked, pouring lemonade into two glasses.

"Sure," he said.

"So, what's up? Spill the beans. Is it your mother?" Jennifer couldn't think of Prue without feeling a pang of guilt.

"No, it's not about her," he said, looking into the distance. "I think I may have made a mistake." He was fiddling with something in his jeans pocket. This wasn't like him.

"What sort of mistake?" Could the dip in the financial markets be that bad?

"You know. By moving in with Emma."

So that was it.

"I miss you," he stammered. "And I miss the children. I want our family back."

He might have thought of that when he abandoned us, she thought. She remained silent while her brain whirred. She felt a huge weight of tiredness descend on her. She was fed up with coping on her own, even with Philippe's help. Was she so desperate that she'd take Jonathan back?

Jonathan slid her a sideways glance and reached out to touch her hand. She pulled it away.

"I'm sorry, Jonathan," she said after a brief silence. "But it's too late."

He gave a sigh, a sigh of anger, not of sorrow. Was he angry with her for refusing to get back together? Same old Jonathan, winding her up about something that was his fault.

"OK," he said brusquely. "I can see there's no point in discussing it."

She was starting to feel upset. Jonathan always shied away from discussing his feelings, and she knew how much it would have cost him to say what he had. But she couldn't help him. The fact was she no longer loved him.

"You're right," she said.

They heard the sound of a car.

"That'll be Pippa," said Jennifer. "She said she'd come over after dinner."

The car door slammed. Jennifer got up and called to her, waving. Jonathan and the dog followed.

"I'm off," he said.

"You're still taking the kids on Saturday morning, aren't you?" Jennifer asked.

"Of course."

He nodded at Pippa and went to his car without another word.

"Come over here," Jennifer said to Pippa. "We were just having a drink outside."

Pippa watched Jonathan depart then raised her eyebrows. When Jennifer didn't answer her unspoken question, Pippa pointed at a bank of hydrangeas. "You should take pictures of your garden for the France in Bloom competition. It looks gorgeous."

"Do you think so? Thanks. Maybe I'll send some to Meredith," Jennifer replied. "Lemonade?"

"So, what's up with Jonathan?" Pippa asked, accepting a glass.

"I'm still processing it, to tell you the truth," Jennifer replied. "But, well, in a nutshell, he wants us to get back together. Can you imagine that? After less than a year with that woman."

"Wow."

"Yeah. He told me that things haven't been going so well, and that he regrets moving out, blah blah blah."

"And what did you say?"

"What did I say? I said 'no', of course!" The anger she'd been suppressing finally erupted. "I can't believe how manipulative he is. According to him he wants to move back because he misses the children, but he wasn't thinking about them when he ran off with Emma, was he?"

She took a sip of lemonade and put her glass down so hard it splashed on to the table. She wiped her cheek with the back of her hand.

"I mean — honestly!" she said, shaking her head. "Do you know what's weird? I was looking at him and I could no longer see what attracted me to him in the first place. I mean, we were childhood sweethearts, weren't we? But now I've completely switched off."

"I suppose that's what happened when my husband walked out on me," said Pippa.

"Oh, I'm sorry. I hadn't meant to . . ."

"That's all right. It was a long time ago. And what about Philippe?" Pippa asked.

"Exactly! Jonathan, the selfish bastard — who is probably jealous, mind — expects me to drop Philippe just like that. Well things aren't that simple, are they?"

"I guess not," said Pippa.

"And at that point, you arrived, thank goodness." She shook her head. "What do you want to go to Kerivac for, anyway?"

"Ah, well. That's what I need to explain." And Pippa told her what she had seen.

Jennifer's eyes widened. "Jean-Michel? Do you think it's his garage, not Seznec's? Tanguy Seznec is the one who lives there."

"How would I know?" Pippa said. "But first we need to check that the motorbike is the missing one and not one belonging to Jean-Michel or Seznec. I couldn't tell if it was a vintage one or not from where I was standing."

"Yes. I see," said Jennifer. "But how do you mean to go about it? Are you suggesting we break in? We can't do that."

"How else are we going to find out?" said Pippa. "Report it to the police? What if we're wrong? We'll look like a couple of silly busybodies. It's only an old garage in a quiet back alley. I'm sure it won't have a burglar alarm or anything, it looked pretty shabby to me."

Jennifer took another sip of her lemonade. "You haven't mentioned it to Yann then?"

Pippa shook her head. "Not yet, no."

"Hmm. If you're right, this could be a big deal." She thought for a moment. "OK. Let me just make sure Mariam's all right to keep an eye on Luke for a bit. Then I think we'd better ask Philippe to help, if he's willing. One of us will have to be a lookout, and he'll have a toolbox and might know how to open the door. What sort of a door is it?"

"It's one of those metal doors with a handle you used to see in the sixties, the ones you push up to open," said Pippa. She no longer seemed quite as confident as when she'd arrived. "But you're right, let's ask Philippe. Maybe he can meet us there?"

Jennifer pulled a face. "I'm not sure how he'll feel about doing a break-in, but I'll give it a try."

They looked at each other and giggled nervously as the reality of what they were setting in motion began to sink in.

CHAPTER 34

Half an hour later, Jennifer and Pippa arrived in Kerivac, parked some distance from the menhirs and made their way on foot to the alleyway. They found Philippe examining a red garage door.

"This is the one, yes?"

"Yes," said Pippa. She nudged Jennifer and suggested she mount guard at the end of the alley. Jennifer, who looked on edge, gave her a grateful smile.

"I hope Seznec doesn't show up. He might recognise us from the *fest-noz*," she said.

Philippe finished his inspection of the door. He wrinkled his nose. "I'm not a locksmith, you know. I can't think of a way to open this lock without breaking it."

Pippa felt defeated. Had they come here for nothing?

"Maybe with a screwdriver?" she ventured.

"*Pff*," he said. "Ah, but wait." He stepped forward and, stretching himself to his full height, began feeling along the top of the door.

"I think a skewer will do it," he said with a smile as broad as a Breton dam.

"A what?"

"The door has got a lever inside," he explained. "I'm a cheesemaker, remember? Do you know the secret of blue cheese? For the *affinage*, I use a skewer to pierce the cheese and let the air in."

"And?"

"*Et voilà*, that is what turns the interior blue!"

"No. I mean, what's that got to do with opening a garage door?" said Pippa.

"Ah," said Philippe, noticing her impatience. "It just so happens that I have some skewers in my car. So, if I push one through here," he pointed to the gap at the top, "I might just be able to pull on the safety release."

At that moment, Jennifer began waving frantically, and they heard the distinctive rattle of a diesel vehicle drawing near. Jennifer crouched down between two rubbish bins just before it turned the corner, while Philippe and Pippa ran to the end of the alley where he'd parked. They got into his car just as an Audi appeared. The driver stopped at the first garage and a young man in jeans got out, pushed open the door and drove the car inside. Her heart palpitating, Pippa prayed he wouldn't look in their direction. He came out, shut the door and strolled off.

Would he spot Jennifer? Where *was* she? Pippa screwed up her eyes and stared at the bins where she'd seen her crouch down, but she didn't seem to be there.

As soon as the man had finally disappeared, Pippa left Philippe searching for his skewers in the car boot and returned to the garage door. Jennifer re-emerged, looking a little dusty, and resumed her post. Philippe, having found a skewer, was straining to manoeuvre it inside the gap. After a few tense moments, they heard a satisfying click.

"Ca y *est*," he whispered. "Quick now."

He raised the door. Pippa went inside and whipped out her phone. She took several pictures of the black vintage motorcycle while Philippe fiddled with something at the top of the door.

"Ready?" he hissed. She had a moment's doubt — had they done the right thing by involving him? What if he was caught breaking into a private garage? She ducked outside and gave Jennifer a thumbs up. Philippe went to his car, while Pippa followed Jennifer, only now thinking to check that no one was looking down at them from a bedroom window. She was relieved to see that the high wall along the alleyway hid them from sight.

She joined Jennifer in the car, and they gave each other a triumphant high five.

"And was it?" Jennifer asked, indicating Pippa's phone.

"The Brough? Look." She held the phone out to Jennifer.

"Phew. Thank God," said Jennifer, switching on the ignition. "Lawrence of Arabia would be proud of us."

CHAPTER 35

"Let's get out of here," said Jennifer, accelerating away and throwing Pippa back against her seat.

"Thank God Seznec didn't turn up," she said, checking the rear-view mirror once again.

Pippa grabbed Jennifer by the arm. "I've just had a thought. What if he and Jean-Michel are working together?"

"That's impossible," Jennifer said. "They can't stand each other. They came to blows at the *fest-noz*, remember?"

"Oh yes. Damn. I'd forgotten about that."

Only when they reached the main road to Louennec did the two women begin to relax. Pippa looked out of the window at fields that sped past in a blur, drumming her fingers on her thigh. It would take her another fifteen minutes to get home because she'd left her car at Jennifer's.

"So, what was Jean-Michel doing in that lockup if he isn't involved?" she said after a while.

Jennifer, checking the mirror again, gave a shrug. "I've no idea. It makes no sense."

"I'm going to ring Vicky," Pippa announced. "We should tell her we've found the bike."

She took out her phone and listened while Vicky delivered a stream of words that Jennifer couldn't make out.

Finally, Pippa said, "I see," and, "good luck with that," and rang off.

"What was she saying? Why didn't you tell her about the Brough?" Jennifer demanded. She turned into Louennec and drove slowly through the village.

"You'll never believe this. She told me she's just discovered that Alex sold it just before he died."

"Ah, so that would explain why it was in that garage. And we risked being caught breaking in for nothing," Jennifer said with a sigh.

"Actually, no. Because — get this — she said it was sold to a guy in Ireland," said Pippa.

"What?" said Jennifer, while the car swerved. "A guy in Ireland?"

"She says she's let the gendarmerie know," Pippa went on. "And now she has to apologise to Seznec, who she reported to the police. Poor Vicky."

"So, what on earth is going on?" Jennifer moaned. "What is that damned bike doing in a lockup in Kerivac? I don't understand any of it!"

CHAPTER 36

It was haymaking time, and Pippa drove home past fields of bales wrapped in plastic resembling giant hair curlers. Sunflowers drooped in the cool of evening.

She resolved to confess to Yann, but how to do it without admitting to the break-in? She always had to tread gently with him for fear of stepping on his toes — professionally speaking — and provoking a row.

When she pulled into her drive she saw that Yann's downstairs light was on. At ten o'clock not only was it too late to go round, but also time for her to go to bed, since she had to get up at four. But her brain refused to switch off. She prowled round the house tidying up, collecting old newspapers for the recycling bin.

She went outside and began throwing the papers into the bin. Yann came out at the same moment, possibly disturbed by the noise. They stood, each on their doorstep, illuminated by the street light.

"Fancy meeting you here," she said.

"*Les grands esprits se rencontrent*," he said with a grin. She didn't know the French for *great minds think alike*, but it had to mean that.

"*Un pousse-café?*" he asked. But she knew that if she had a nightcap she'd never get to sleep.

"It's too late for me, I'm afraid. How about dinner tomorrow?"

"Good. Come to mine. I've got langoustines from the fishmonger."

"Wonderful. *Bonne nuit.*"

* * *

The next evening, the two of them ate langoustines on Yann's patio. Pippa, rather dubiously, watched to see how he went about it. Soon, however, she was tearing them apart with her fingers and sucking at the heads with gusto.

"That was delicious," she said, throwing the last head on to her plate. None of her British friends ever ate more than the tail, discarding the rest.

"More wine?" he asked. She nodded and he refilled her glass with Gros Plant.

"Yann," she began. He narrowed his eyes. "I know something about Alex's stolen motorbike."

"The Brough?" He pronounced it "bro", which almost made her laugh.

"Yes. I think it's pronounced 'Bruff', actually. As in wuff wuff." Why was she saying this?

"Are you talking about the sale?" he asked.

"No, though Vicky told me about that. The thing is . . ." she hesitated, "that I, er, happened to see the motorbike in a garage in Kerivac, where Tanguy Seznec lives."

"Peeper, I told you. We have ruled him out of the theft."

"Yes, but did you check his garage?"

This was a mistake. She ought to know better than to insinuate that the police might not be doing their work properly. He frowned.

"If you remember, I told you we checked his premises, which naturally includes his garage. His motorbike was there, and I can assure you that it's not a . . . a *Bruff.*"

"OK," Pippa went on. "But what if I tell you that I took a picture of the bike inside the garage. I can show you if you want."

His frown deepened. "And what were you doing there, might I ask?"

"I told you. I was painting in Kerivac." So far she hadn't told a lie. She took her phone from her pocket.

"Look."

He took the phone and stared at the photo, zooming in on it.

"I see that this photo was taken from *inside* a garage," he said. She felt like crumpling. How could she tell him the truth? She'd be implicating Jennifer and Philippe in a crime. She decided to brazen it out.

"OK. So it may not be Seznec's garage. I don't know which one is his, but the one I'm talking about has a red door. It's about halfway along. And before I took the picture, I saw Jean-Michel, the first deputy mayor, going inside."

To her surprise, Yann didn't get angry. After a silence that seemed to last an age, he said, "Thank you, Peeper. This is very interesting."

CHAPTER 37

On a sunny summer's day the market was a delightful sight. Jennifer took a moment to admire the colourful wares on display. Solenn was back with her Breton jewellery, which was evidently a hit with the tourists. Jennifer noticed Pippa wave to her competitor, the one selling rustic loaves, who pretended not to have seen her. Philippe, serving a slice of Brie to a customer, looked across and gave her a wink. She smiled back. They were taking advantage of the children being away with Jonathan to see each other in the evenings.

She saw a small woman with a helmet of black hair walking purposefully past her stall looking the other way. After a moment of uncertainty, Jennifer recognised Mme Seznec, Tanguy's wife and the mother of the girl who had bullied Mariam. Mme Seznec had been one of Jennifer's customers until she had confronted her about the bullying. She gritted her teeth at the memory.

"Look at those tomatoes!" The voice belonged to Meredith, who was gesturing at the summer fruit and vegetables heaped on Jennifer's stall.

"There's plenty more where they came from," she said with a smile. "How are things?"

"Oh, the usual," Meredith said. "Why are the French so negative? Every time I suggest doing something at a council meeting, the response is always 'no'. They don't like change. And Sylvie is always the most vociferous. I wish I could get rid of her."

"But at least the flower competition application is going ahead, isn't it?"

Meredith frowned. "Yes, but too slowly for my liking. The cycle path is almost finished, but the residents need to spruce up their gardens. I'm still nervous about marauding villagers who might spoil everything just as we're putting the application together. And thank you for your lovely pictures, my dear."

"You're welcome. If you need me to take any photos for the application, let me know," Jennifer offered. "By the way, did you know it was the Seznec family who defaced the menhirs in Kerivac with anti-flower show graffiti?"

"That man! What's wrong with him?" she muttered. "They're yobs, aren't they?"

Jennifer became aware that customers were lining up behind Meredith, and asked her if she wanted any tomatoes. She bought a kilo and a bunch of gladioli before making her stately way through the market, shaking hands with her constituents as she went.

Jennifer was packing up her stall when she heard someone clear their throat behind her.

"Do you have any eggs left?"

Jennifer turned and recognised Vicky's cook.

"Hello. You're Bleuzenn, aren't you?"

The woman nodded. She wore no make-up and her eyes had the same fine lines in the corners as Pippa's own. *We must be the same age,* she thought. "It so happens I do. How many do you need?"

"Six would be fine. But if you have more . . ."

"I think there may be almost a dozen." She rifled around in her car boot and took out a carton.

"There's nine here. They're Marans. Will that do?"

"*Super.*" The woman took out some change and placed the eggs carefully in her bulging shopping bag. "I need them for Madame Vicky."

"How's everything at the château?" Jennifer asked. She didn't often see Bleuzenn, who lived in one of the outlying villages.

"Well . . ." said Bleuzenn. Jennifer sensed she wanted to unburden herself. "I think we'd all be better off if Tanguy Seznec got another job," she said, and closed her lips firmly.

"Why's that? Do you mean over the stolen motorbike? I thought he was in the clear," said Jennifer. She certainly wasn't going to mention the lockup in Kerivac.

"In the clear? I don't understand why he's not the main suspect!" She gave an irritated sigh. "Tanguy was always asking Monsieur for a raise. He refused, of course, because Tanguy is lazy and hangs around with all the wrong people. But we could all see that he was getting angrier and angrier."

"Seznec? So, you mean he had a motive for stealing the bike. Revenge on Alex."

"Of course!" Bleuzenn almost shouted. "He wanted to hurt Monsieur. And how best to do it? Steal his best motorcycle. Isn't it obvious?"

"Did you tell Madame Vicky about this?"

Bleuzenn shook her head. "I didn't, actually. Do you know, she called in all the staff and interviewed us. As though I was a suspect! I was so surprised I didn't think to mention Tanguy's demands. But I did tell Madame that if she wanted to know who was stealing, she should look in his direction. He was the only one of us who was interested in motorbikes."

Her look was fiery with indignation.

"Anyway, next thing, all of us staff were called into the gendarmerie because she had referred the case to the police. And I made sure I mentioned Tanguy to them. But I don't know if they did anything about it. I mean, *il n'y a pas mort d'homme.*" Nobody died.

Except they had, Jennifer thought.

Bleuzenn's eyes met Jennifer's and she added, embarrassed, "Apart from Monsieur, of course. And Monsieur Pierre." She looked around at the few remaining market stalls. "Did Peeper leave already?"

"Yes. She had to go back to the bakery. She's very busy at the moment." Jennifer was sorry to miss their usual catch-up in the café. There would have been so much to say.

"I'd better get going myself," said Jennifer. "But I'm seeing Vicky this afternoon at the Vieilles Charrues, and I'll tell her what you said."

Bleuzenn put a finger to her lips. "Please, don't mention my name."

"Of course not." *This is the way the village gossip spreads,* Jennifer thought. *Everyone at loggerheads with everyone else, but never a name spoken.*

CHAPTER 38

Jennifer got out of the car and heard the pulsing sound of rock music from across the fields. She knocked on the solid oak front door of the château. Vicky, holding a plastic container, was dressed for the music festival in a pair of torn black shorts, a heavily studded belt and a pair of Doc Martens. Safety pins held together the holes in her sleeveless T-shirt, her bare arms blackened with tattoos. Her hair, dyed orange with henna, stuck out in all directions. Jennifer, in jeans and a linen shirt, felt out of place and underdressed.

"You're sure you want to do this? I mean, scatter his ashes at a public festival?" Jennifer asked her.

"Of course. It's what he would have wanted. I'm saving the rest to take back to England."

"Hmm," said Jennifer. "I wonder if that's allowed these days?"

Vicky shot her a defiant look. "Who cares? I'm taking them anyway."

Vicky put the container with the ashes into her backpack and they set off for the festival on foot. The château was located behind one of the campsites provided for festivalgoers, so it wasn't far, and a lot easier than driving.

"How are you coping, Vicky?" Jennifer asked as they walked along the lane towards the campsite. Underwear was drying on tent guy lines, flapping like flags in the gentle breeze.

"Easy," Vicky said, flashing a brisk smile. "I self-medicate." She counted on her fingers. "Pills to get to sleep, and pills when I get up. I do uppers and downers and God knows what else. I'll tell you what, though, my dreams are amazing."

"You should be careful," Jennifer said. "Have you thought of seeing a grief counsellor? I mean you've had a double whammy, haven't you, what with Alex and then Pierre . . ."

"Nah. Therapists aren't my thing. I'm OK," Vicky insisted. "I don't need sympathy from anyone, including those hypocrites in Alex's family. They're only after his money. Well, they can just eff off!"

"You're not talking about his children? What, the two who came to the funeral?"

"I certainly am. All lah di dah, wouldn't harm a fly, but I'm telling you, they're sharks underneath," Vicky said. "And as for their mum, that Sharon, she's the worst of the lot!"

They joined a queue at the festival entrance and security checked their bags. The box in Vicky's backpack went unnoticed, the attendant probably assuming it to be a large vegan lunch pack. Inside, they pushed through the crowd to stand in front of the main arena.

Jennifer felt somewhat nervous about the gathered fans' reaction to what Vicky intended to do. "What's the plan, Vicky? Where are you going to scatter the ashes?"

"I thought either beside the stage, or at the foot of a tree. What do you think?"

"I'd say beside a tree, it'll be much easier," said Jennifer. "I mean, were you going to drop Alex into the mosh pit? Imagine what people would think!"

Vicky made it clear that this was the wrong answer. Jennifer was obviously far too boring and conventional.

"Come on," said Vicky, pushing her way through the metalheads in the main stage audience towards the head-bangers in the mosh pit, and the full force of the Breton

Clangers. Jennifer recalled Vicky telling her that the band had been inspired by Alex. Jennifer felt increasingly incongruous as around her, people jumped up and down, crashing into each other. Most held a bottle of beer in one hand. How many of them were on drugs?

When they were nearly at the stage, Vicky began to dance. Swaying to the beat, she pulled off her backpack and opened the plastic container. Her arms shot into the air, and she released a cloud of grey ash. The fans nearest her backed away, staring in amazement at the middle-aged rock chick with the bright orange hair whirling faster and faster, her face smudged with tears and ash. Jennifer, meanwhile, wished she were anywhere but here. Why had she agreed to accompany her? She might have known what it would be like. She wondered if Vicky was on something, if she'd taken a pill before leaving the house. Vicky danced on, almost losing her footing, as the rhythm intensified.

After what seemed an eternity to Jennifer, the song reached its climax and the audience applauded. Some of the fans clapped their hands to Vicky, who stumbled over to her, panting.

"Well done," said Jennifer, catching hold of her before she fell. "Alex would have been proud of you." *Let me out of here,* she thought.

Vicky bent over and put her hands on her knees while she regained her breath.

"That's it then," she said brightly, standing up straight again. "Job done. Shall we go home for a cuppa?"

They made their way slowly through the happy crush — young and old, Bretons and foreigners.

As they retraced their steps past the campsite, Jennifer asked Vicky if she'd heard anything more about the police investigations.

"Like I said, I've given up on ever finding out who killed Alex," she began. "As for Pierre, I'm waiting to hear the results of forensics on the gun that shot him. At first they seemed to think he shot himself, but now they reckon it might have been staged."

"Really? How do they know that?"

"They asked me whether Pierre was right-handed. I said no, he was left-handed. So, it's a bit suspicious that he was holding the gun in his right hand. Clever, eh?"

Jennifer nodded. They walked on in silence, each buried in her own thoughts. The electric gates to the château slid open soundlessly and they entered the grounds.

"Did you know that your handyman had asked Alex repeatedly for a raise before he died?" Jennifer said suddenly.

Vicky stopped dead and stared at her. "Tanguy? No, I didn't. Alex would have kept that to himself. Most likely he didn't want the staff to find out; they'd only be jealous. Who told you anyway?"

"Oh, just something I overheard people talking about in the village," Jennifer said.

"And here was I about to apologise to him for accusing him of stealing Alex's motorbike. Did you know it's in Ireland now?"

Jennifer hesitated. Should she tell her about the lockup? "It's not. It's in a garage in Kerivac, where Tanguy Seznec lives."

"What? That's a marmalade dropper! Why are you only telling me this now?" Vicky let her backpack fall to the ground and wiped her face with her arm.

Jennifer explained what she and Pippa had seen.

"Did you tell the gendarmerie?" Vicky demanded.

"I think Pippa is having a word with Yann. It seems Tanguy was already under investigation for the extremist violence in the village."

Vicky exploded with rage. "Right, that does it. I've had it up to here" — she brought the back of her hand to her chin — "with that man and his sodding nose ring, his greasy rat's tail and far-right pals. I'm going to sack him."

Jennifer attempted to say that Jean-Michel had been seen at the lockup, but Vicky silenced her with a gesture.

"He's not even a decent workman. I always have to go round after him when he's fixed something in the house. In fact, I don't know why I haven't fired him long before now. He owed his job to Alex, and now he's gone there's no reason to keep the little bastard on."

Exhausted, Jennifer said nothing. Vicky was too much for her. She'd done her duty, and didn't want to get embroiled in her complicated affairs. At the door, she opened her bag to look for the car keys.

"Coming in for that cuppa?" Vicky asked.

"Actually, no thanks. I've got stuff to do at home, so I'd better get going."

Vicky walked with her to the car. "By the way, do you know what else the gendarmes told me?"

Jennifer cocked her head, listening.

"They found two other guns at Pierre's house."

"Two? That's interesting," said Jennifer, her eyes wide.

"Yes. So I guess it's possible that the gun in his hand wasn't his. Or maybe they can get an ID from the fingerprints on it. Anyway, that's the story so far."

CHAPTER 39

The problem with Pippa's bakery was that she was fast becoming a victim of its success. She needed to have a discussion with Gwen.

As soon as she got back from the market, she went into the back where she found Gwen making packets of sandwiches for the Vieilles Charrues.

One of the things that was beginning to bother Pippa was the phone app offering leftovers that customers picked up at the end of the day. It had been Gwen's idea to get the app, which let people pick up a lucky bag for a fixed rate of four euros, giving them a saving of a few euros on the surprise items.

"Can we have a quick chat?" Pippa asked.

"Of course, madame."

"You know this app we've got. Well, I've noticed that people are coming in and asking what's in the bag."

Gwen flushed.

"I'm not complaining about you," said Pippa, "but about the customers. This isn't how it's supposed to work. The idea is that they should take what they're given. I think that in future, we're going to have to point that out to people who say they don't want a *pain aux raisins* in the bag, or whatever. They shouldn't be negotiating what they get."

Gwen nodded and went into the back. Pippa took up her position at the counter. The bottom line was that she was starting to feel like she was losing control. There was more and more work because of the catering orders, which now came in regularly, but financially she still couldn't afford to take on a second full-time member of staff. In any case, the bakery was too small. All she could manage was the occasional part-time helper, who prepared canapés and delivered them to customers. Yannick, the young part-timer, had already taken a vanload of picnic sandwiches to the Vieilles Charrues that morning. And then in a few days' time, the Tour de France would be coming through. Another opportunity for the bakery. But the thought didn't make her happy.

Pippa went to the display and began rearranging the cakes. At the window she caught sight of a wispy young woman passing in front of the bakery, and waved to her. It was Nathalie, the widow of the man who had sold his hemp field to Pierre. Her house was across a field at the back of the bakery.

Pippa stepped outside and said, "*Bonjour.*"

"*Ça va?*"

"*Ça va. Et vous?*"

"*Ça va.*"

The customary exchange completed, Pippa asked Nathalie if she had found work since the death of her husband, Didier. They had a young daughter who often stopped at the bakery on her way home from school to pick up bread and sometimes an apple turnover.

Nathalie said she'd got a job as a teaching assistant at the village primary school. Pippa realised she wouldn't be earning much.

"Do you wish you hadn't sold the hemp field?" She refrained from asking whether Nathalie was raising her daughter on her own — after all, it was only a year since her husband had died.

"Not really, no," she replied. "It gave us some cash when we needed it, and in any case the land couldn't be developed, so I couldn't have got any more for it unless the *mairie* changed the zoning."

"You could have got a lot more if you'd planted cannabis in the middle, like Pierre did," said Pippa with the beginnings of a smile, adding quickly, "It's very sad about him shooting himself, isn't it?"

"Shooting himself? *Pff.* Is that what they think?" Nathalie looked sceptical.

"What makes you say that?" Pippa asked.

Nathalie hesitated for a second. "What I know is that after he was caught by the gendarmes, Pierre told me he'd have to stop selling his crop to the dealers. He had to, didn't he? Some people think that the dealers went after him to punish him."

"Really? Do the police know about this?"

Nathalie shrugged. "How would I know?"

Just then, Pippa spotted another customer about to enter the shop.

"Anyway, I'd better get to work," said Nathalie, following Pippa's gaze. She walked off, and Pippa returned to her post inside the bakery. She couldn't wait to tell Yann.

CHAPTER 40

Her face in her hands, Meredith sat at her desk in the *mairie*, staring at her computer screen.

The anonymous message on the *mairie* website was clear and concise, accusing her, in French, of being a *foutue Anglaise* who was riding roughshod over the villagers. She was used to seeing this sort of criticism on social media. What she didn't expect was to read that she deserved to be packed into a coffin, in order to follow her husband into the cemetery.

Her first reaction was to laugh. This person wasn't serious, surely. She read it again, and it struck home. This was a death threat! Had she really become that unpopular? She wondered again whether Sylvie Le Goff had been stirring up animosity to the "effing English" mayor.

She glanced at her office door, which was closed. Sylvie always left for home the minute the workday ended, never staying later, no matter how much remained to be done. What was she going to accuse her of, anyway?

She picked up the phone and rang her ally, Jean-Michel. As soon as she heard his voice, she felt as though she could burst into tears. "Do you have a moment?"

"What's the matter, Meredith? Is there a problem? I can call at the *mairie* on my way home if you like," he said. "I need to pick up some bread anyway."

"No, don't worry. I just wanted to tell you that I've received a death threat via the office website. I've never received one before, and I don't know what to do."

"*Putain!*" he exclaimed. "Nowadays this is becoming a thing in France, you know. Thanks to social media, people think they can insult their mayors with impunity, even though you are working on their behalf. I've heard of some mayors resigning because of this."

"Really?" said Meredith.

"Did you see what happened in Callac?" he said.

"You mean the Callac near here?"

"Yes. The mayor of the *commune* and his councillors received all sorts of threats from the far right, who were against the establishment of a migrant centre in the village."

"I thought the mayor backed down on that project."

"Yes, he did," said Jean-Michel. "But that didn't stop the extreme right. It's like a cancer in our society. Did you hear about that other mayor in a village outside Nantes who resigned after his house was set on fire?"

"Was that the far right too?" Meredith asked.

"Yes, of course. Those cases are a bit different from ours, because the protests were triggered by their opposition to migrant centres. The situation here is not so obvious. The flower war in our *commune* is only part of the problem. But the result is the same, I'm afraid."

Meredith frowned and looked again at the message on her computer screen. Did she have to wait until her house was set on fire before she reacted?

"Well, I've had enough! I'm going to resign."

The line went silent. "Are you there, Jean-Michel?"

"Is this about Sylvie? You can't let her win."

"No, it's not just about her," she said more calmly. "Of course not. I've been thinking about it for some time. This job isn't what I thought it would be. I thought we'd be able to join together to stop them building new wind farms, but the *préfet* carried on regardless! I'm an elected mayor but I have no power. Whenever I try to do something to improve the *commune*, I get nothing but insults. Look what's happened to my plans to apply for *ville fleurie* status. And now I'm getting death threats! I've had enough, Jean-Michel."

Her voice trembling, Meredith held back a sob of self-pity.

"Let's deal with that first," he said. "You must take a screenshot of the message, and then we will report it to the gendarmerie. They must investigate."

"And what good will that do?" she said.

"I know what you mean. But we must follow the protocol. If we don't file a complaint, the situation could escalate."

"That's what I'm worried about," said Meredith. "What happens if it gets worse, like in the other *communes* you mentioned? I've already had somebody daub *Rosbifs Go Home* on my garage door, but this is a serious threat. I'm telling you, I'm really thinking about stepping down. I can't take another four years of this."

"I believe that you are a very good mayor. You have the interests of the *commune* at heart. But the village is polarised. Society is polarised. You know that."

"Yes, of course," she said. "And that's why I'm thinking of resigning. I'm deadly serious."

"Listen, Meredith," said Jean-Michel. "If you go, I go. It won't be the first time that a mayor and councillors have been forced to step down. But for now, I beg you, do what I say. We must do everything we can to find out who is behind this hate campaign."

CHAPTER 41

Jennifer had prepared a pasta dish for their first family meal together since the children returned from a week's holiday with Jonathan.

Pervenche was upstairs with Mariam. Jennifer was glad she was back in the picture — having ditched the "boyfriend" before the school holidays — as she'd found Ivy rather coarse and far too loud. Who knows what trouble Mariam would have got into if they'd continued being friends?

Luke clattered downstairs and into the kitchen as soon as she called. Philippe had set the table. The children seemed to be getting used to his presence, particularly Luke. Mariam regarded him with the same wary expression as she gave everyone else.

Jennifer and Philippe had spent every night together while the children were away. The next milestone — or obstacle — would be if or when he moved in.

"Tell me about Ploumanach," Philippe said to Luke. "*Les rochers rouges.* Did you like it?"

"Yes. Do you know what we did? We went snorkelling. It was great."

"Wasn't it a bit dangerous?" Jennifer asked.

"Yeah!" Luke replied. "Romy was scared!"

Jennifer hadn't been told that Emma and her daughter were going with them. Her leg twitched involuntarily, colliding with the dog under the table.

"She wasn't in your tent, was she?" Jennifer asked.

"No," Mariam said. "She and Emma had one next to ours."

"And Daddy had his own tent?"

Mariam glanced at Luke before replying with a nod.

Jennifer stirred her spaghetti and broccoli thoughtfully. So they'd never actually split up, had they? What a coward Jonathan was. And how convenient for the pair of them that he had his own tent.

Manfully, Philippe kept the conversation going.

"So, are you looking forward to the Tour de France next week?"

"Yeah!" said Luke.

"I'm staying here," Mariam announced, wrinkling her nose in distaste. "Me too," said Pervenche. "Cycling is boring."

"But it's the first time they've been anywhere near Louennec. You'll see, it's lots of fun," said Philippe. "We need to get there early, take some folding chairs and sit by the roadside, so we'll be there when the caravan goes past. You'll get sweets and presents. Did you know that?"

"Do they have Haribos?" Luke asked.

"I'm sure they do," Philippe replied with a smile.

"I want to be a cyclist when I grow up," said Luke.

"Good for you," said Philippe. "You know that Bernard Hinault from Brittany was a very famous Tour de France cyclist?"

"Of course I do. I've seen the statues of the riders in Carhaix," said Luke.

"Oh, I see you're an expert," said Philippe.

"I thought you wanted to be a farmer," said Jennifer. She stood up and began to collect the plates.

"Keep up, Mummy," said Luke.

"OK, so that's settled then, is it? What about you, Mariam? What are you going to do if you're not coming with us?"

"Dunno. Go to Pervenche's place?" She glanced at her friend, who nodded.

"Is that OK, madame? My mother can pick up Mariam. And we'd like her to come with us on holiday next month."

This was the first Jennifer had heard of this, but she wasn't displeased.

"Of course. Where are you going? Don't your parents have a place in Nice?"

"Outside Nice, yes."

"Good. So that's settled then," said Jennifer. "Have you mentioned this to Daddy?"

The children said they had. They got up amid a great squeaking of chairs on the stone floor.

"Just one more thing," Jennifer added. "Mariam, I want you and Luke to make yourselves scarce on Saturday night because I'm having a drinks party for us oldies, and I know you don't like being press-ganged into helping out."

"Can I take the bike to Alain's?" Luke asked.

"Of course. It'll be good practice for the Tour de France," Jennifer said.

CHAPTER 42

It was after midnight when Pippa was awoken from a deep sleep by the ringing of the phone.

Vicky. Something must be up. Vicky knew that Pippa always went to bed early because of the bakery.

As she went to answer the call, she heard a low rumble that seemed to be coming from the main street of Louennec.

"Pippa, something terrible's happened!" Vicky screamed. "I fired Seznec, and he's gone on the rampage."

"What's he done?"

"He took the mini digger out of the barn and drove it into the rose garden. He's dug up all my rose bushes, the bastard! The noise woke me up. Erwan is going to go apeshit when he finds out!"

"I'm sorry about that, Vicky, but I don't quite see—"

"The thing is, after that he set off down the lane towards Louennec. I'm scared he's going to dig up every single garden! He's gone totally batshit crazy!"

"OK. I'm on it," said Pippa, hanging up. Her first thought was to alert Yann. She threw on some clothes and went outside to see if there were any lights on at his house. There were, so she phoned him. He picked up straight away.

A couple of minutes later, they were both running down the street in search of the digger. It wasn't hard to find. The noise had awoken the whole village. Lights were being switched on and dogs were barking. Pippa caught sight of Seznec driving the machine down a side street, followed by two or three villagers, including a bald man in pyjamas, slippers and a dressing gown, who was yelling profanities.

"There he is!" she shouted to Yann. "He must be going to the Charpentiers' house. They're the people he had a row with at the *fest-noz*."

Taking out his phone, Yann ran ahead. "Leave it to me, Peeper," he called back. "By the way, very good piece of information about the drug dealers. It could change everything."

What could he mean? She followed at a distance and saw Yann reach Seznec just as he was angling the bucket's claws into the soil, ready to rip up a flowerbed. Suddenly Jean-Michel, Seznec's old sparring partner, appeared from round the corner and ran at him, spoiling for a fight. Jean-Michel tried to climb up into the cabin of the digger, but Seznec pushed him back. The handyman had a big smile on his face as though he was having the time of his life.

Yann grabbed hold of Jean-Michel and pulled him away. He showed his ID to Seznec and began remonstrating with him, watched by a small crowd of villagers, all in their nightwear. Seznec, still defiant, nevertheless handed over the keys to Yann and stepped down from his cab.

"*C'est un fouteur de merde, ce mec-là!*" one of them said to Pippa as she joined them. Her French was good enough for her to understand that they were definitely not on Seznec's side, and thought him a shit-stirrer.

"We've had enough of him and his neo-Nazi mates," said Michel, the owner of the bar-tabac next to the bakery. His face, always red, was redder than ever. He greeted Pippa like an old friend, even though they hardly knew each other. "Louennec was a quiet village until those rockers arrived," he grumbled.

Everyone stepped back as a flashing blue light announced the arrival of reinforcements from the gendarmerie in Carhaix. Two gendarmes got out and ran over to Yann, who, ignoring Seznec's insults, was filling out a form.

The lights had gone on in the upstairs windows of the house where the digger had come to a halt, and a couple of minutes later, the Charpentiers appeared at the front door. The young woman, in a flimsy nightdress, and her husband in boxer shorts and a T-shirt, began yelling a stream of invective at Seznec. They went briefly inside to find something to cover themselves with before re-emerging to join in the general pandemonium.

The bystanders exchanged views on what would happen to Seznec.

"He'll be done for *tapage nocturne*," said one. "He's obviously been disturbing the peace."

"Yeah. He'll probably get off with a fine," said Michel. They watched as the two gendarmes led Seznec away and put him in the back of their car.

Pippa had seen enough. She had to get back to bed or she would suffer tomorrow. She told Michel to give her best wishes to his wife, Solange, and gave Yann a farewell wave. But he indicated that he wanted to leave with her. He cordoned off the digger and turned to the small group of people still hanging around. "That's it. Nothing to see here. Good night, everyone."

He and Pippa walked slowly back to their cul-de-sac.

"Will he really escape with a fine?" she asked.

"Maybe, maybe not. Remember, he damaged private property at the château. And before he got to the Chemin du Lys, he'd already dug up another couple of gardens. What an idiot. He risks being sent to jail."

"Good riddance. Didn't you manage to pin anything on him from the search of his house? All this might have been avoided if you'd caught him then."

"Actually, no. Anyway, now we can nail him for disturbing public order, he was caught red-handed at that."

When they reached Pippa's door, Yann took her face in his hands. "I wanted to thank you, Peeper. Now we're on the trail of the drug dealers suspected of killing Pierre, the investigation is going in a completely different direction."

"Really? Which direction is that?"

He touched his nose and grinned. Then he kissed her goodnight. "You'll have to wait, but probably not very long."

CHAPTER 43

Out in the garden the shadows of the lime trees crept like dark tongues across the grass. Jennifer stood at the back door, gazing upon it in satisfaction.

She'd changed out of her customary jeans and boots into a long skirt and sandals. Philippe had helped her set up a couple of trestle tables on one side for the food, and arranged some folding chairs around the perimeter in case Meredith and others wanted to sit down. He'd cut the grass the day before, without being asked. She couldn't help comparing him to Jonathan, who'd always considered gardening to be a menial task well below his pay grade.

The guests were beginning to arrive, and she ushered them into the garden, where she'd strung Chinese lanterns above the pink hydrangeas along the fence.

"Just help yourselves, everyone. The wine's in the fridge or on the kitchen table, and the food's over there," she said. The nibbles mostly consisted of pâté spread on to slices of baguette. Philippe had provided an entire Brie.

Philippe made a beeline for Solenn as soon as she and Derek arrived, and they began an animated conversation in French. Solenn was wearing one of her Breton necklaces featuring the three-legged triskele symbol. Jennifer decided it was high time she supported her friend by buying one for herself.

Pippa and Meredith both arrived at the same time. Meredith collapsed on to a chair, fanning herself with one hand.

"It's hot, isn't it?" she said.

"Shall I move this chair into the shade for you?" Pippa offered.

"Everything all right, Meredith?" Jennifer asked, joining them.

"No, it's not!" she exclaimed. "That man Seznec has single-handedly wrecked our application for the France in Bloom competition. The landscape architects who'd been helping us unfortunately chose this week to come back, and saw the damage for themselves."

"Oh no! Isn't there anything that can be done?" Jennifer asked.

"It doesn't look like it. I mean, it was pretty obvious that the villagers aren't united behind the scheme, so they advised us to hold off. We can always try again. But I can't bear the thought that Sylvie has won!" Pippa and Jennifer murmured in sympathy. "I had a council meeting last night, at which we discussed the whole thing. I felt sorry for Jean-Michel, because he did a great job with the application. And when I looked across at Sylvie Le Goff, she was smirking. I could have hit her!"

"So, you reckon Jean-Michel is a good guy, do you?" Pippa asked with a glance at Jennifer.

"Well, naturally," said Meredith. "Remember he switched sides to support me in the elections, risking becoming unpopular in the village. And he really puts his back into his work at the *mairie*, which is great when you think he's got a busy job at the freight company. In fact, the other day, when I received my first death threat" — Pippa and Jennifer stared at her, open-mouthed in surprise — "Jean-Michel said that if I resigned, he'd leave too! That shows you how loyal he is."

She stopped speaking and looked at each of them in turn. "Why? What made you ask?"

Pippa gave a Sphinx-like smile, asked if either of them wanted a refill, which they declined, and disappeared among the guests.

"Is Yann coming?" Meredith asked Jennifer.

"He told Pippa he'd try to come along a bit later, but it depends on his shift," said Jennifer.

"Such a nice man. And so discreet," said Meredith.

"But what's this about a death threat?" Jennifer said.

Meredith waved a hand in the air. "I've grown used to being insulted, it goes with the job. But that took the biscuit. Some horrible person posted a message on the *mairie*'s website threatening to kill me. They said it was time I joined Craig in the cemetery."

"Oh, how awful!" Jennifer exclaimed.

"Yes, and when I told Jean-Michel that I wanted to resign because of it, that's when he said he'd walk out too."

Derek joined them, giving Jennifer a chance to see to the other guests. Going to the kitchen in search of some chilled wine, she heard voices coming from the living room. She took out a bottle of Gros Plant from the fridge and was intrigued to see Vicky and Yann deep in conversation.

She went back into the garden, where Philippe and Solenn were still chatting in French. She took the bottle across and gave each of them a top-up. "We were just talking about how the market has changed. There are more tourists and food trucks now. That is new," Philippe said rather hesitantly in English. It wasn't immediately clear whether he thought this was a good thing or not.

"We can speak in French, you know," she said. "Isn't that down to the Vieilles Charrues? It's put Carhaix on the map, hasn't it?"

Solenn nodded. "Yes. It's good for business, definitely."

"It's such a pity that Louennec isn't going to take part in the France in Bloom contest. That would have meant more visitors too, don't you think?" said Jennifer.

"Aren't we going ahead with that?" said Solenn. Philippe, too, looked surprised.

"Meredith just told us. Unfortunately, the officials from Quimper came over to inspect the village just after Seznec had laid waste to the place."

"*Quel con*," said Philippe, shaking his head.

"Oh, what a shame," said Solenn. "My hydrangeas are magnificent this year. Thank goodness we are too far outside Louennec to be affected by village politics."

"It's terrible for Meredith," said Jennifer. "She feels that her authority has been undermined. And it gives more ammunition to Sylvie Le Goff, who thinks she's running the place anyway."

"*Pff*, what a dreadful woman," said Solenn. "She stuck her nose into my jewellery business when I began selling online. She really hates private enterprise — the English too," she added, with a wink at Jennifer. The French still seemed to think that jokes about "*perfide* Albion" and Joan of Arc — burned at the stake by *les Anglais* — were funny.

"I used to think she was just the mayor's secretary when we first moved here. But now we know the truth," said Jennifer with a bitter laugh. "She's a civil servant and practically unsackable."

Yann and Vicky emerged through the back door together. He went over to greet Pippa, while Vicky approached Jennifer.

"Can I get you anything?" Jennifer asked, looking at her anxiously. "Are you OK?" Vicky, dressed in black as usual, her hair a vibrant orange, was swaying slightly. "Is it the heat?"

Vicky reached out and held on to Jennifer's arm.

"No. It's something Yann's just told me. It seems they know what happened to Alex's motorbike. I can't believe it."

"What?" Jennifer asked. "You mean they've solved the mystery of the lockup?"

Vicky nodded. "Yes. If I understood him correctly, there's going to be an announcement later tonight."

CHAPTER 44

Vicky's grip on Jennifer's arm tightened.

"Can't you tell me? It's going to be public knowledge soon anyway," said Jennifer. "Come on, let's go inside."

They went into the kitchen. Jennifer went straight to the fridge and took out a bottle of wine. She poured two glasses and they seated themselves at the table. "OK," she said. "Go on."

"According to Yann, they've arrested the thief, and you'll never guess who it is — Jean-Michel. He was Alex's friend! How could he do such a thing?" said Vicky, her voice trembling with emotion.

"But how is that even possible?" said Jennifer. "He couldn't have taken it from your garage because he didn't have a key. Anyway, I thought Alex sold the bike to somebody in Ireland."

Vicky took a long swig of wine. "Yes, he did. He asked Jean-Michel to take care of sending it on — natch, because he's in that business. After Alex died, Jean-Michel must have realised that nobody needed to find out that the bike never made it as far as County Cork. I suppose he fobbed off the buyer with some cock and bull story—"

"Rented a lockup—"

"Exactly. In Kerivac, not Louennec, so that it was out of the way. I guess maybe he thought he'd sell it off later, when people had forgotten about it."

"I see. Clever," said Jennifer.

"Diabolical, if you ask me, darlin'. He confessed the whole thing to the police after they traced the garage to him. He couldn't get away with it then, could he? I reckon the gendarmerie did a bloody good job there," said Vicky.

Jennifer smiled. It was the first time she'd heard Vicky actually praise the cops.

"So, it definitely wasn't Seznec then?"

Vicky shook her head. "No. He just happened to have another garage in the same alleyway, where he keeps his own motorcycle."

"Poor Meredith," Jennifer said. "She was just telling me how much she relied on Jean-Michel, and what a help he was."

"Well, shit happens," said Vicky. "But Yann told me something else as well. Promise you won't say anything?"

"Of course. What?"

Jennifer had her back to the door, so she didn't notice Philippe come in.

"Hi, Philippe," said Vicky.

He touched Jennifer lightly on the arm and asked her where she kept the cornichons.

"Oh. They're usually in the fridge but there's a new jar in the cupboard. Let me get it for you."

"Don't worry, I'll find it," he said, opening cupboard doors. The two women watched him in silence. He found what he was looking for and held up the jar.

"Thanks," he said and went back outside.

Jennifer turned back to Vicky. "Sorry about that. You were saying?"

Her eyes on the kitchen door, Vicky lowered her voice. "Yann said they've arrested two drug dealers on suspicion of murdering Pierre. I knew he didn't kill himself! The poor guy must have told them he couldn't sell them any more cannabis after the police discovered his crop."

"Sounds like a rather over-the-top reaction on their part — if it's true," Jennifer said.

"They're drug dealers, vermin. That's exactly how they'd react. Pierre was losing them money, so they lashed out and made it look like a suicide. Bastards."

She leaned forward. "Anyway, Yann told me to expect a further development in the next few days . . ."

CHAPTER 45

It was just after lunch. Bleuzenn was putting some biscuits in the oven while Vicky cleared away her dishes, when they heard someone bang on the front door.

"All right, I'm coming," Vicky said, drying her hands on a Breton tea towel. "There's no need to wake the dead."

She went to the door and looked through the peephole. Two gendarmes in uniform stood outside. One was Yann, the other she didn't recognise. Could this be the development Yann had spoken of at Jennifer's party? She opened the door.

Yann introduced the second gendarme as Major Guillaume Le Gall, who shook her hand and said he was head of the *brigade de gendarmerie* in Carhaix. She wondered why such a senior officer had come to see her. His round face was inscrutable. This must be serious.

"*Vous parlez français?*" Le Gall enquired.

"*Couci-couça,*" she replied, tilting her hand. "So-so."

She led them into the dining room with a mounting sense of foreboding, and asked them to take seats at the oak dining table. She sat in her usual place overlooking the once impeccable flowerbeds.

"*Un moment*," she said, and went into the kitchen to collect her phone. She showed them the translation app, which caused some hilarity.

Le Gall cleared his throat. Vicky pointed to the phone and he began, "Madame, we are here to tell you that we have identified the murderer of your husband, Alex 'Rockface' Johnson."

She listened while his words were repeated in standard English.

"Oh, my God," she said, staring at him in amazement, and almost forgetting to use the app. "After all this time! This is quite unexpected."

"Thanks to forensics, we have ascertained that his killer was Pierre Lambert."

Vicky struggled to comprehend what she'd just heard.

"Pierre? My Pierre?" She shook her head in disbelief. "You're kidding me. That's impossible! How do you know that?"

Speaking slowly and gently, Le Gall explained that forensics had determined that the two bullets which fatally wounded her husband had come from Pierre's rifle.

Vicky jumped up and went to the window, where she turned to face them. "But what about the ballistics tests? You people told me that none of the hunters who were there that day had fired the fatal shots! This is ridiculous. You've got it all wrong!"

She sat down again, scowling at them, her bright hair glinting in the afternoon sunshine.

The two men looked at each other. Le Gall spoke into the app. "Madame, the rifle was found at Monsieur Lambert's house. It was not the weapon he used during the boar hunt."

He paused for a moment, to make sure Vicky was digesting the information, before continuing: "We believe that he intended to kill your husband during the hunt, and for that purpose he took two rifles with him. After he shot Monsieur Johnson, he had time to conceal the murder weapon in his car and return with the second rifle, which he gave to the gendarmes when they arrived."

Vicky listened to the English version from her phone with mounting distress, but said nothing.

"And what is more, the murder weapon was unlicensed. There is no doubt about the conclusion. We wanted to let you know before we inform the public. Your husband had many fans, who will want to hear who murdered him."

Vicky held up her hand. "Hold on, hold on. Wait a second. This makes no sense. Pierre was my lover. Why on earth would he want to hurt me?"

"Unfortunately, madame, we cannot ask him that. As you know, he was not a rich man. It is possible that he believed that with your husband out of the way, his, er, relationship with you would make him a wealthy man."

Vicky sat back and folded her arms. "Well, I don't believe it."

"I should say that it was only after we realised he had been murdered at his property that we carried out the forensic examinations. Otherwise, it is possible that we would never have established the truth."

"Truth!" she spat out. "I'm telling you I knew my Pierre, and he would never have done such a thing."

Le Gall shrugged. "You may think what you like, madame, but in our experience, people behave in — what shall I say — unexpected ways when money is at stake. You are, after all, a very wealthy lady."

Vicky stood up, putting a hand on the table to steady herself. "I think you'd better go."

CHAPTER 46

It was a long time since the people of Louennec had had so much juicy gossip to chew over.

The arrest of Jean-Michel — a deputy mayor, no less — had stunned the *commune*. And the news that one of their own, Pierre Lambert, had murdered Rockface before himself being killed by drug dealers, had made its way through the village at lightning speed.

At the bakery, Pippa listened with some amusement to the conversations of her customers while they waited to be served.

"*Oh là là*, that Pierre! He was after her money of course," a woman said. "And, don't forget, he was younger than her."

"Have you seen what she looks like? A scarecrow," another whispered. "What could he have seen in her?"

Over the past few days, Pippa had spent hours with Vicky, who was devastated by Pierre's betrayal. It had taken some time for her to accept that the police investigation had reached the correct conclusion. But how could she argue with the results of the ballistics test proving that Alex had been shot by Pierre's unlicensed gun?

Yann, concerned about Vicky's reaction to the news, asked Pippa over dinner how her friend was doing.

"She'll be all right in the end, I think," Pippa said. "But she's grieving all over again. It's tough for her, all on her own."

"What will she do?" he asked.

"I expect that she'll probably move back to England. There's no reason for her to stay now. I've told her to take her time and not to do anything rash."

"That's good advice, Peeper," he said. "And it was thanks to you we solved the crime."

She grinned. "Not only that one, but the mystery of the missing motorbike too!"

CHAPTER 47

On a day of brilliant sunshine, the Tour de France came to town.

The *peloton* was due to pass through Louennec at around 1 p.m., but everyone wanted to be there for the publicity caravan. Thanks to the merchandise tossed into the crowd, this part of the event provided just as much excitement, so people had gathered a good hour before the riders appeared.

Jennifer set up their folding chairs on a bend in the main road, thinking it would provide a good vantage point to take pictures from. Luke was chattering away to Philippe about the various cyclists' form. Jennifer was impressed with his French, as well as his knowledge of the sport.

"You've done your homework," she said to him.

Philippe gave him a brief history of the caravan. "Did you know the caravan parade joined the Tour in 1930?" he said, while Luke listened wide-eyed. "In those days, it brought consumer goods to the people in rural areas like this — shampoo, and things like that."

"You mean they didn't have shampoo?"

"No, and no washing powder either," said Philippe with a laugh.

Pippa, who was sitting next to Jennifer, had brought a picnic hamper. Just as she was opening it, Meredith came to join them.

"Sure you've got enough?" Meredith asked.

"There's plenty, don't worry," Pippa said. "Find a seat. I'll just get the paper plates out, then you can serve yourselves."

Further down the road, a food truck from the market had set up shop. Banners advertising local stores rippled in the breeze on the roadside. People were eating picnics beside their parked cars, and a trail of campervans stretched as far as the eye could see. Some of the spectators had draped themselves in the French flag. Meredith was waving to people from her chair. One elderly man had come prepared for a long wait, and was sitting on a folding chair drinking a beer and reading *Le Télégramme*.

Meredith helped herself to a ham sandwich.

"Are you doing all right?" Jennifer asked her in a low voice. "I know you were upset about Jean-Michel."

"I was, of course," she replied. "I felt betrayed, but also I was disappointed that he was so greedy for money that he'd do a thing like that. What's more, I'll have to find someone to replace him on the council. And he was my main ally there." Meredith's eyes, hooded from tiredness and stress, fell on a group of people sitting on the other side of the road. "Oh, my God. Look who's here."

Jennifer, pouring tea from a thermos, saw Sylvie Le Goff directly opposite them. She was accompanied by a thin man, presumably her husband, but also by two or three of the metalheads who had been at the *fest-noz*. Could they be her sons?

Sylvie stared at Meredith for a moment, before giving her a brief nod and turning back to the man at her side.

"I can't stand that woman," said Meredith through gritted teeth.

"We've obviously chosen a good place to sit," Jennifer said.

They waited for the excitement to begin, whiling away the time munching on sandwiches. They soaked up the festive atmosphere until the first floats of the parade appeared over the brow of the hill.

"La Caravane! It's here!" cried Luke, jumping to his feet.

"Careful now. Stay off the road," Jennifer warned, taking him by the arm. "I mean it. It's dangerous. And no selfies, remember."

"All right, all right," he muttered. Everyone was on their feet, waving at the girls on the floats to attract their attention. "*Par ici! par ici!*" Luke yelled, and was immediately pelted with packs of sweets, T-shirts, sun hats, key rings and pens, all of which he gathered up feverishly. He turned to Jennifer with a beaming smile. "This is the best thing ever!"

It didn't take long for the novelty to wear off, however. "How much longer till the cyclists get here?" he asked Philippe.

Philippe laughed. "Oh, only another hour."

At last, the clatter of a helicopter announced the first riders. They came over the brow of the hill, surrounded by an entourage of cars and motorbikes.

"Here they are!" cried Luke, jumping to his feet again. Everyone around them was standing with their phones in the air, preparing to capture the historic moment.

To loud applause from the spectators, the leading cyclists tore down the slope and around the curve, followed by the *peloton* in a blur of colour.

"Look out for the yellow jersey," Philippe advised Luke.

The spectators screamed and shouted as the riders sped by. What followed next seemed to take place in slow motion. A cyclist hurtling down the slope touched the man next to him, who slewed to the left, braking sharply and heading straight for Sylvie Le Goff and her group. The riders behind crashed into them. One rider somersaulted off his bike into the crowd, while others careered wildly, out of control.

Horrified, Jennifer covered her eyes. When she opened them again, she saw, on the other side of the road, a tangled heap of bikes and bodies. Sylvie Le Goff, her legs splayed, had been pinned to the ground beneath two bikes whose upturned wheels spun uselessly in the air. Her face was turned towards Jennifer, her painted eyebrows raised in her trademark expression of surprise.

THE END

ACKNOWLEDGEMENTS

My special thanks to Mike Gray, Katie Haigh Mayet and Brigitte Vallée, and, as ever, to my wonderful editors at Joffe Books.

THE JOFFE BOOKS STORY

We began in 2014 when Jasper agreed to publish his mum's much-rejected romance novel and it became a bestseller.

Since then we've grown into the largest independent publisher in the UK. We're extremely proud to publish some of the very best writers in the world, including Joy Ellis, Faith Martin, Caro Ramsay, Helen Forrester, Simon Brett and Robert Goddard. Everyone at Joffe Books loves reading and we never forget that it all begins with the magic of an author telling a story.

We are proud to publish talented first-time authors, as well as established writers whose books we love introducing to a new generation of readers.

We won Trade Publisher of the Year at the Independent Publishing Awards in 2023. We have been shortlisted for Independent Publisher of the Year at the British Book Awards for the last four years, and were shortlisted for the Diversity and Inclusivity Award at the 2022 Independent Publishing Awards. In 2023 we were shortlisted for Publisher of the Year at the RNA Industry Awards.

We built this company with your help, and we love to hear from you, so please email us about absolutely anything bookish at feedback@joffebooks.com

If you want to receive free books every Friday and hear about all our new releases, join our mailing list: www.joffebooks.com/contact

And when you tell your friends about us, just remember: it's pronounced Joffe as in coffee or toffee!